'I've chosen the right woman for my wife.'

'Your pretend wife,' she corrected.

'That's what I said.'

'Not exactly.'

'You like to have the last word, don't you?'

'I'm a woman, Mr Montgomery.'

'I did notice *that*, Miss Valentine.' He watched her cheeks blossom with pink. 'And while I am but a humble man—' he ignored her soft snort '—I'm a determined one. Our paths *will* cross again, Emma. And again. Until I have your agreement that becoming my pretend wife benefits everyone.'

Her mouth moved, but no words emerged. He smiled and stepped out into the hall. 'I'll see you later.'

He pushed his hands into his pockets and thought about the woman on the other side of the door. She was perfect for his needs. He just needed to remember that his needs were *strictly* business. That her curvy body, from slender neck to trim ankles, was off-limits.

All he needed was a *pretend* wife.

Dear Reader,

Welcome to six, substantial, satisfying Silhouette® Special Editions!

THAT'S MY BABY! is our ever popular spot where readers can always find a story with a baby at the centre of the action and this month Allison Leigh gives us *Millionaire's Instant Baby*—there's a linked story next month from Laurie Paige, too.

We're halfway through Muriel Jensen's WHO'S THE DADDY? series with *Father Formula*, and the remaining answers to any questions about the identical triplets come in *Father Found* in December.

Penny Richards, who used to write for us as Bay Matthews, starts her latest trilogy with *Sophie's Scandal* and the reunion of a father with the mother of his secret child. Then there are two lost boys needing help in Sherryl Woods's latest AND BABY MAKES THREE novel, so it's lucky Michael Delacourt knows a lady friend to call!

A Child on the Way is a new Wilder family romance from the very talented and experienced pen of Janis Reams Hudson, while *Warrior's Embrace* is Peggy Webb's second terrific novel for Special Edition™ and has a sexy Sioux hero who needs to find the right woman!

Happy reading!

The Editors

Millionaire's Instant Baby

ALLISON LEIGH

™ SILHOUETTE
SPECIAL EDITION
®

*First published in Great Britain 2001
Silhouette Books, Eton House, 18-24 Paradise Road,
Richmond, Surrey TW9 1SR*

© Harlequin Books S.A. 2000

Special thanks and acknowledgement are given to Allison Leigh.

ISBN 0 373 24312 X

23-1001

*Printed and bound in Spain
by Litografía Rosés S.A., Barcelona*

For my own Prince Charming.
Happy anniversary.

ALLISON LEIGH

started early by writing a Halloween play that her school
class performed. Since then, though her tastes have
changed, her love for reading has not. And her writing
appetite simply grows more voracious by the day.

Born in Southern California, she has lived in eight different cities in four different states. She has been, at
one time or another, a cosmetologist, a computer pro-
grammer and an administrative assistant.

Allison and her husband currently make their home in
Arizona, where their time is thoroughly filled with two
very active daughters, full-time jobs, pets, church, family and friends. In order to give herself the precious writing time she craves, she burns a lot of midnight oil.

A great believer in the power of love—her parents
still hold hands—she cannot imagine anything more
exciting to write about than the miracle of two hearts
coming together.

THAT'S MY BABY!

Heart-tugging stories about the littlest matchmakers—as they find their way into a family's welcoming arms!

THE BABY LEGACY by Pamela Toth
August 2001

When an anonymous sperm donor tries to withdraw his 'contribution', he learns a beautiful woman is eight months pregnant—with *his* child!

WHO'S THAT BABY? by Diana Whitney
September 2001

A Native American lawyer finds a baby on his doorstep—and more than he bargains for with an irresistible paediatrician who has more than medicine on her mind!

MILLIONAIRE'S INSTANT BABY
by Allison Leigh
October 2001

Pretend to be married to a millionaire 'husband'? It seemed an easy way for this struggling single mum to earn a trust fund for her newborn. But she never thought she'd fall for her make-believe spouse…

MAKE WAY FOR BABIES! by Laurie Paige
November 2001

All she needed was a helping hand with her infant twins—until her former brother-in-law stepped up to play 'daddy'—and walked right into her heart.

Chapter One

"I'm looking for a wife."

Emma Valentine turned her attention away from the tall man who'd just made the flat statement and focused on the feel of the unfamiliar, wonderful weight of the baby in her arms. Her son, barely one day old, took her breath away. All the months of waiting, of worrying, of planning. All were wrapped within the soft blue blanket, contained in the eight pounds of perfectly formed baby. She drew her finger along his velvety cheek, not wanting to wake him, but unable to resist touching.

"Miss Valentine, did you hear me?"

She bent over and pressed her lips ever so gently against her son's perfect forehead. Her son. She straightened when the door behind the man swished open and Nell Hastings, one of Emma's favorite nurses, appeared to take the baby back to the nursery.

Emma reluctantly surrendered Chandler. And only after the door had swished closed again did she turn her attention back to the man.

Her arms felt woefully empty, and she folded them across her chest, painfully aware of the sight she must present to the man who looked so flawless he could have stepped from the pages of a men's fashion magazine. She shifted gingerly in the cushioned side chair and wished she had more clothing covering her than her pink chenille bathrobe and pale hospital gown. "I'm sorry. Mr....?"

"Montgomery. Kyle Montgomery."

Emma nodded. Dennis Reid, the chief of staff at the Buttonwood Baby Clinic, had introduced him when he'd stopped by. Obviously Dr. Reid had come by with the intention of introducing this man to Emma, though she couldn't fathom why. Up until now, Emma's only contact with Dr. Reid occurred when the man went into Mom & Pop's. The diner where she waitressed was located across from the medical complex and she knew a lot of the clinic's staff.

She studied the man standing in her room, from the cuffed hem of his black pleated trousers that broke ever so perfectly over his gleaming leather boots to the white shirt flowing over an impressive set of shoulders. The button at his throat was unfastened, but Emma figured he probably had a tie in his car or his briefcase. She knew instinctively that this was a man who'd been born wearing imported suits and silk ties. Even his chestnut hair had fallen precisely back into thick waves when he'd raked his fingers through it.

"Dr. Reid was saying something about you needing assistance with a job?" she asked. It helped to look in the vicinity of his ear, she decided, rather than into his starkly handsome face. Because then she didn't feel quite so much like a wrung-out dishrag in the face of his masculine elegance.

"I don't know how I can help," she went on. "As you can see, I'll be busy for the next little while, and after that..." She trailed off.

After that it was back to her two jobs and the worry about paying the hospital bill. She'd already determined that the tuition for her next semester of college courses would have to wait.

"I believe we can help each other, Emma."

She swallowed the dart of nervousness that rose when he crossed the room, passing the other bed—empty for now—before pulling out the chair opposite her.

Almost as if he recognized her reaction, he seemed to consciously relax his rigid stance. He sat, rested his arms on his thighs. Clasped his long fingers together. Almost smiled, but didn't quite make it. "As I was saying, I need a wife. A family."

Good gravy, he smelled nice.

The thought shocked her. She moistened her lips. "Mr. Montgomery, I really don't know what you—"

"Kyle." He halted her confused words. "And I can explain. But it's occurred to me that this isn't the best time. You're tired, and my offer might be better received after you've had some rest."

"Mr. Montgomery..." Emma tugged self-consciously at the lapel of her robe, then flushed when his startling green gaze followed the movement of her hand. She'd been blessed, as her mama termed it, with a curvaceous figure by the time she'd turned fourteen. Becoming pregnant and having a child had only increased the problem.

She swallowed and tried again. "Kyle, I really can't imagine how I can help you find your family. But you might as well tell me what's on your mind now, because I'll be leaving the hospital this afternoon and I—"

"Already?" Lush black lashes narrowed around his intense gaze. "Surely you're not up to being released yet."

She wondered if she'd accidentally been given some type of drug other than acetaminophen, because this was surely the oddest conversation she'd ever had. Mr. Mont— *Kyle* seemed distinctly annoyed. As if he suspected she was receiving inadequate care. "Women don't spend days and days in the hospital anymore when they give birth, Kyle. I'm healthy, as is my baby. Everything went just fine." Thank heavens. "And studies show—"

"I wasn't casting aspersions on the medical care you're receiving. I was just surprised." He sat back in his chair, laying one arm on the minuscule table beside it. Emma had the strongest impression he was mentally drumming his fingers against the tabletop. "Right. I apologize for the timing here, but Dennis Reid seemed to think you might be able to help me, and I'm running short of time."

"Do you think I know your wife? What is her name?"

"I don't already *have* a wife, Emma." He hesitated for a fraction of a second. Just long enough to make her stomach drop to her toes. "I *need* one. And I'm hoping you'll be her."

Thank goodness she was sitting. Because if she hadn't been, she'd have ended up on the floor. "Mr. Montgomery," she said firmly, "I don't know what Dr. Reid led ya'll to believe about me, but—"

"I'm going about this wrong." He sat forward again, bringing with him that tantalizing scent of expensive aftershave. No drugstore brands for this man. He was strictly the charge-by-the-quarter-ounce type.

He linked his fingers together again, regarding her with eyes that gave no hint of the manic mind he must possess. "Dennis said I could count on your discretion."

He seemed to be waiting, so she nodded hesitantly. The call button was just out of her reach, but if she leaned to the side, she could probably get to it. She would get to it, because she was a mother now. She *would* protect her child with every fiber of her being, and that meant she also had to protect herself. Even from a sinfully attractive madman.

"I run ChandlerAIR," he continued calmly. "Have you heard… Yes, I can see by your expression that you've heard of us. I'm in the middle of some delicate negotiations with a company we are acquiring. The founder of this company has some old-fashioned ideas about how he likes to do business." Kyle paused, as if she needed a moment to digest what he was saying.

She nodded, since she didn't know how else to respond.

Kyle's lips twisted slightly and he turned his attention to his hands. "He refuses to deal with anyone who is not the fine upstanding family man he is," he elaborated. "Acquiring this other company will benefit ChandlerAIR, but it will also help the economy here in Buttonwood. Provide jobs. Increase tourism—"

"I understand the economic benefits, Mr. Montgomery. Surely this other man would understand that, as well, wouldn't he?" She brushed back a lock of hair and was dismayed to realize her hand was trembling.

"Payton Cummings is perfectly happy to retain control of his company as long as he needs to until he finds the right opportunity. The right—"

"Family man," Emma murmured.

"Exactly." Kyle's lips tightened for a brief moment. "I'm more determined to see this acquisition through than Cummings is. Assuming the trappings of a family man is something I'm prepared to do to attain my goals."

"But…but why me? Someone in your company, your girlfriend…"

"I don't have one."

Men who looked like Kyle Montgomery always had a woman in the background somewhere. Whether they admitted it or not. She swallowed the bitter thought.

"I don't have time in my life right now for personal entanglements," he was saying, his voice deep and smooth. "And I don't want to create any ties with my associates that might later cause discomfort."

"Discomfort," Emma repeated. It was the word so often used to describe childbirth to prospective parents. She considered it singularly inadequate to describe the reality. "But with me, a total stranger, there would be no cause for later…discomfort."

"Essentially, yes. I'm new to this area, Emma. I've bought a house and I'm moving ChandlerAIR's corporate offices from Denver. Having a family that lives here dovetails nicely with what Cummings already knows about my plans."

"Then he probably already knows you're not married."

"He doesn't." There was no room for doubt in his assurance.

She argued, anyway. "You can't know that. I've seen articles now and then about your company. About the services you offer and its success." Phenomenal success, if Emma recalled correctly. She also recalled his company being praised particularly for its progressive policies toward its employees. "I'll be the first to admit that I don't follow the business pages very closely. But even I know a little about your company. A man you're plannin' to do business with like you've described would obviously know a great deal more. Including some personal details."

Kyle nodded. "Those are valid points. But until last year when he moved to Durango, Cummings had been living in New Mexico. Our paths didn't cross. Besides which, I've always kept my private life private. Only my closest associates know much about me personally. I prefer it that way."

Emma couldn't imagine it. There were times she

suspected every resident of Buttonwood knew the
business of everyone else. It was almost as bad as
her hometown in Tennessee. "But to suddenly produce a wife? I just don't see how you can possibly
hope to fool anyone."

His eyes narrowed. "I can count on your discretion, can't I, Emma?"

She winced. "As if anyone would believe me if I
went around announcing that a guy like you walked
into my hospital room one morning and asked me, a
simple waitress, to be his wife."

He frowned. "For appearances only," he corrected. "I meant no offense. This is a delicate situation. Cummings already thinks I'm married. But
he's been showing more interest in that area of my
life, and I'm going to have to introduce him to my
wife, I feel certain, before he'll close the deal."

"You told him you were married because he
wouldn't do business with you otherwise?"

"I told his stepdaughter I was married when she
came on to me at our first meeting."

"Oh," Emma murmured.

Kyle grimaced. "I didn't want to jeopardize my
plans. It seemed, at the time, the easiest way."

"And you couldn't have just said you didn't want
to mix business with pleasure?"

"Let's just say that Winter Cummings is a determined woman who doesn't necessarily hold with her
stepdaddy's values."

Kyle's hand moved and Emma realized he was
unclenching his fist.

"Ironically, once word reached Cummings that I'd
been recently married, he was willing to meet with

me himself. I wasn't going to derail the deal by getting into explanations.''

She was believing every word that left his lips. He was utterly serious.

And his seriousness seemed far more dangerous than his being nuts. ''Perhaps Mr. Cummings and his crew aren't the type of people with whom *you* want to do business,'' she suggested faintly.

Kyle smiled tightly. ''I want Payton Cummings's company,'' he said. ''If it takes a family to get it, I'll produce a family. At least for show.''

Emma swallowed. ''But to…to marry strictly for the purpose of a business deal? That seems so, well, extreme, don't you think?''

''It wouldn't be a real marriage,'' he said. ''I just need you and your son to pose as my family. The two of you would move in with me—strictly business,'' he assured when she caught her breath audibly.

''But, sugar, it would be a lie.'' Her face heated as the words burst out.

Kyle felt an odd stirring when he let himself look at the young woman opposite him. Her melodic voice had been growing increasingly smooth, like warm honey. There was more than a touch of the South in this dark-haired beauty. He'd had women call him all sorts of nicknames from darling to pig, but he knew he'd never been a *sugar*. He dragged his thoughts front and center, where they belonged. ''I have to consider the weight of what I'm trying to accomplish.''

''Ah.'' She nodded, her big brown eyes studying

him steadily. "The old 'end justifies the means' reasoning."

"I want to add more flights, Emma," he said truthfully. "More flights, more service, more employees. The only people who will be hurt if ChandlerAIR's acquisition of Cummings Courier Service falls through at this late date will be the considerable number of people within the Four Corners area who *won't* be able to work for me. That's four states, Emma. Colorado, Utah, Arizona and New Mexico."

"I did pass geography, Mr. Montgomery. And regardless of your motives, it still doesn't make lyin' right."

His jaw hardened. He'd had this argument with himself too many times already to want to sit here and go through it with this young woman. He'd spent too many years planning. Waiting for just this opportunity. To finally take the action that, while it wouldn't reverse the past, would go a long way toward evening the score.

If producing the family Payton kept harping on got Kyle to his goal, then produce a family he would.

ChandlerAIR would survive if the deal to acquire CCS didn't go through. His company was strong and solid because he'd devoted his existence to it for most of his adult life. But taking over CCS was an action that went beyond business.

And he had no intention of discussing his personal motives with this young woman, no matter how honeyed her voice. "I prefer to look at it as expedience. And perhaps we should agree to disagree on the point," he said.

"Might be wise," she murmured, shifting in her chair.

A fine white line appeared around her softly compressed lips at the movement, and he felt a jab of conscience. She'd just had a baby. Sitting here arguing ethics was undoubtedly the last thing she'd expected to be doing today. "Miss Valentine. Emma. Give my offer some thought." He kept his voice calm even though his impulse was to push the issue. "I'll make it worth your while."

Far from calming her, however, her face blanched. "I'm sorry, Mr. Montgomery." Her tone said she was anything but. "I can't help you." Her hands curled over the sides of the chair and she pushed herself gingerly to her feet.

He rose, automatically reaching out to assist her, but the frosty look she gave him had him keeping his hands to himself. He felt awkward and inept, something he hadn't experienced for at least twenty years. Yet watching her slowly maneuver herself to the hospital bed without offering assistance went against his grain.

"One of my sisters had a baby last year," he said.

"How nice," she murmured.

It would have been so simple just to lift her off her feet and deposit her on the bed—much easier than watching her efforts to climb into it. He looked away, shoving his hands in his pockets. When his sister had been in the hospital after giving birth, her room had been filled to overflowing with flowers, plants, balloons and assorted baby gifts. The only thing personal in this room was one small green plant with a cheerful smiley-face balloon sticking out of it.

At the rustle of sheets he let his gaze travel back to her. Emma was still bundled in the thick robe and looked as if she'd just as soon be buried in it as remove it with him present.

This wasn't going at all the way he wanted. Needed.

He started to reach up to loosen his tie, then realized he'd left it in his car, so it wasn't a tie that made him feel choked. "Is someone picking you up this afternoon to take you home?"

She folded her arms across the top of the sheet and sighed faintly. "You're not going to go away, are you."

It hadn't been a question. He answered, anyway. "Emma, this is too important for me to go away." How many times had he removed an obstacle from his path simply because of his ability to outlast, outthink, outmaneuver?

Only this time, the obstacle in Kyle's path had smudgy shadows beneath her eyes and slender shoulders he was certain were being held straight through sheer grit. "But I can see you're exhausted. So I'll come back later when you're released and get you settled at home. We can discuss this more then."

"There is nothing to discuss. Besides, I have my car here and I'll be getting myself and my son home just fine."

"Your car is here? Did someone drop it off for you?" He pulled his hands from his pockets and wrapped them around the metal rail at the foot of her bed. Kyle had specifically asked Dennis Reid if there was a man in the picture with Emma Valentine. Reid had assured him that Emma was totally on her own.

The last thing Kyle needed was some love-struck fool bumbling onto the scene.

"I drove it here," she said, surprising him into forgetting the issue of her single status.

"While you were in labor?"

"Yes," she said with exaggerated patience. "And I'll drive it home again this afternoon. I assure you I have the proper baby seat and everything, so stop frowning."

"You have no one you could have called on?" If not the man responsible for her pregnancy, then a friend. A sibling. Someone.

Her lips firmed. "Whether I do or not is hardly your business, now is it?"

Kyle would have liked to debate that point, considering he was determined this woman would be his make-believe wife. But there was a loud rattle out in the corridor and the door swished open to reveal a young man in pristine white bearing a breakfast tray.

The orderly smiled genially at them, set the tray on a rolling cart and slid it neatly against the side of Emma's bed, turning it so the tray hung over her lap. Then he lifted the cover from the food and left.

As Kyle peered at the bowl of cooked cereal, the puny foil-covered plastic cup of orange juice and a half-burned piece of toast, he thought of the fluffy omelet, crisp bacon and fragrant coffee Baxter had served him that morning. He'd barely taken time to appreciate the food or the way it had been served— on china at the wrought-iron glass-topped table on his patio.

"Are you hungry, Mr. Montgomery?"

"No, why?"

"You're staring at my breakfast like you haven't seen food in a month." She didn't look at him as she peeled back the foil cover of the juice.

"I haven't seen a breakfast that looks like that in more than a month," he muttered. "I'll bring you back something more…appealing."

She took a healthy swallow of the juice, then picked up a spoon which she plunged into the cereal. "I like hot cereal, Mr. Montgomery. Some people do, you know." Her tone slowed like rich rolling drops of syrup. "Even rich folks, I'm told."

He smiled, genuinely amused. "You think I'm a snob."

Her hesitation was barely noticeable. "I can't imagine what you mean."

His amusement grew. "Neatly avoided and you didn't have to lie." Seeing the corners of her mouth twitch as if she was holding back a reluctant smile of her own, he decided it was a good time to retreat. On a high note, so to speak. "I'll leave you to enjoy your oats and whey," he said. "We'll be talking again."

"I don't think so. Our paths are in different neighborhoods. I doubt they'll cross again."

He shrugged easily and headed toward the door. She didn't know him yet, so she could have no idea how wrong she was. He stopped and turned. "Get some sleep after you eat," he suggested. "It'll be a busy afternoon taking your son home. What did you say his name was?"

She tilted her head. "I didn't. Which you know very well."

"He is a good-looking boy."

Her eyes softened like rich melting chocolate. "Thank you. He is beautiful."

"And his name? You've already given him one, I'm sure." He smiled faintly. "I'll bet you had his name picked out when you were only halfway through your pregnancy." She seemed like the type of woman who'd have cherished every moment she carried her child. Very much the way his sister had.

"Four months along," she admitted.

"And?"

She moistened her lips. Hesitated. "My son's name is Chandler."

Kyle absorbed that. "Well. Good name."

"I named him after a very dear old friend from my hometown," she said evenly. "A name I chose months ago, so wipe that smug look off your face."

"Not smug at all, Emma. It's just another indication that I've chosen the right woman for my wife."

"Your pretend wife," she corrected.

"That's what I said."

"Not exactly."

"You like to have the last word, don't you?"

"I'm a woman, Mr. Montgomery."

"I did notice that, *Miss* Valentine." He watched her cheeks blossom with pink. "And while I am but a humble man—" he ignored her soft snort "—I'm a determined one. Our paths *will* cross again, Emma. And again. Until I have your agreement that becoming my pretend wife benefits everyone."

Her mouth moved, but no words emerged. He smiled and stepped out into the hall. "I'll see you and Chandler later."

The door swished closed, but he heard her honeyed voice in the moment just before it did. "Good gravy."

He pushed his hands into his pockets and thought about the woman on the other side. She was perfect for his needs. He just needed to remember that his needs were *strictly* business. That her curvy body, from slender neck to trim ankles, was off-limits.

All he needed was a pretend wife. He'd keep his hands to himself. He'd keep his thoughts strictly on sewing up every last detail of acquiring Payton Cummings's company.

So that when the day arrived that he dismantled every facet of that damned company, he'd have the personal satisfaction of knowing there wasn't one thing Payton Cummings, Sr., could do about it.

Kyle let out a long breath and went in search of a flower shop.

Chapter Two

"Okay, Emma, this one is what we'll use to file for Chandler's birth certificate. Fill in the blanks, sign and leave it in the folder with the others. The state will send you the certificate once it's recorded. You can leave the folder with the nurse when you're released. Okay?"

Emma nodded and waited until the brisk I'm-from-Records-honey woman left. Then Emma looked down at the form and nibbled the inside of her lip. She'd been completing and signing forms for the past ten minutes. Financial forms, affirming that she didn't have medical insurance and including a payment agreement that would take every cent of the pay she earned from her part-time teaching job for the next few years. Medical-information forms regarding the aftermath of childbirth. Even forms to purchase sets of newborn photos.

She'd ordered one eight-by-ten and six wallet-size ones simply because she hadn't been able to resist the first photo of Chandler, his little fists pressed against his round cheeks and a snug blue cap covering his thatch of dark brown hair. But even the photos were an extravagance these days. Signing all those financial forms had brought home with a thump the responsibilities she had to shoulder. Alone.

Which brought her right back to the birth certificate information. She rolled the pen between her fingers, looking at the empty boxes. Mother's maiden name. Location and date of mother's birth. Father's name.

The tip of her pen hovered over that last box. Father. It took much more than biology to make a father. It took love and commitment and dedication.

Yet all she had was betrayal and lies and a twelve-page legal document sitting in the closet of her apartment.

She drew in a breath and let it out slowly. Then she deliberately slashed a line through the father box before completing the rest, and placed the form, along with the others, inside the folder.

She looked at her watch and hoped the nurse came by soon with her release. She didn't believe for one minute that Kyle Montgomery would be returning as he'd said that morning. Why would he?

He had money. He had incredible looks. He could find a make-believe wife wherever he wanted, *making it worthwhile* for some other woman. Personally

Emma had had enough of rich men who thought they could either buy her presence or buy her absence.

The only man she was interested in was the tiny one sleeping in his carrier right beside her.

She looked down at Chandler, feeling tears threaten. Tears of gratitude for his sweet perfection she could happily shed. But tears filled with worry and fear about the days ahead, of managing, getting by—those tears she refused to indulge.

She was twenty-six years old. When her mama was that age, she had five kids. All daughters. Another year and she had six. The year after that, Hattie Valentine had stopped having babies, because her husband went off one night and didn't come back.

A soft knock on the door caught her attention, and she pushed to her feet, tugging the hem of her cotton maternity top over her hips. Nell Hastings smiled and pushed the door wide until it stayed open on its own. "I've got your ride here, Emma." She patted the bright blue wheelchair, her eyes twinkling. "Is that all your stuff in that bag?"

She didn't wait for an answer, but tucked the handles of the big plastic sack that held bottles of water, formula samples and diapers over the back of the wheelchair.

Emma handed the motherly nurse the folder of paperwork and sat in the chair, holding Chandler in his carrier on her lap as Nell pushed her to the sidewalk outside the small hospital. Emma could see her orange car in the parking lot. She swallowed, thinking it was stupid to feel nervous about leaving the hospital. She could do this. She looked down at her sleeping son. She *would* do this. She climbed out of the wheelchair. It wasn't as if she had no friends to support her decisions. To laugh with. To cry with. She just didn't have a husband. And she'd turned down the offers of a ride home from the hospital. She'd start out as she intended to continue. Depending on herself.

"Emma, you and Chandler are going to be just fine. But you get nervous about anything, you just call. Okay?"

"Thanks, Nell. When I'm back at work, I'll treat you to pie and coffee."

The nurse patted her ample hips. "I don't need pie, but I'll take you up on that." She helped Emma with the plastic bag and overnight case before turning the wheelchair around and heading back inside.

"We can do this, right, Chandler?" With the plastic sack slung over one shoulder, the strap of her overnight bag over the other and Chandler's carrier cradled between her arms, Emma slowly headed toward her car.

When she reached it, she had to set everything down on the ground, though, because her keys were buried somewhere in the overnight bag. Chandler was starting to stir, and she moved his carrier onto the hood of her car, humming to him while she dug blindly through her bag.

"Looks like you could use an extra hand."

Emma gasped, automatically closing her arm over the carrier. She looked across the hood of her ancient car to the gleaming late-model sports car against which Kyle Montgomery leaned lazily. Her heart was thudding only because he'd startled her, she assured herself.

"My two hands are quite sufficient," she said, flushing when the words came out sounding breathless. She swept her hand once more through the interior of her case searching, searching.

He tilted his head slightly, his eyes crinkling at the corners. Emma swallowed and pulled the case in front of her, pushing aside the clothing she'd worn to the hospital in her search. She was certain she'd dumped the keys in the bottom of the case.

"You're overflowing there."

She frowned, looking up. Right there, large as life, was her white cotton bra, D cup and all, hanging drunkenly over the side of the case. She hastily shoved it back inside, finally encountered the sharp edge of a key with her fingertip and pulled the set out triumphantly. Without bothering to refasten the zipper of the case, she hurriedly unlocked the car and dumped the two bags inside, rolled the car window halfway down and reached for the baby carrier. From the corner of her eye, she could see Kyle still leaning against his car.

He'd added the tie that had been missing that morning. Looking just as spit-polished as she'd figured he'd look. She swallowed and tried blocking him from her sight as she bent over her baby.

Though she'd practiced fastening the baby carrier into the stationary base that was already in the car, she fumbled the job. Chandler started whimpering and Emma crooned soothingly to him as she tried again. But the latch wouldn't connect.

Painfully aware of Kyle's gaze, which she couldn't seem to ignore no matter how hard she tried, she worked at the carrier again. And again. Chandler started crying in earnest. "Oh, pumpkin, don't," she murmured, trying to distract him with the pacifier the nurse had sent with them. But Chandler wasn't interested in the pacifier, and his newborn wail rose.

The panic rose in her far too easily. Her knees felt wobbly and all she wanted to do was lie down. She took a deep breath and tried fitting the carrier into place once more. What was *wrong* with the thing?

"Let me give it a try."

Emma looked over her shoulder at Kyle, who'd moved to stand behind her. His wide shoulders blocked the bright afternoon sun in a way that no man wearing a silk tie should be able to do. "I can do it."

"I'm sure you can," he said mildly. "But that's the same model I bought my sister when she had her baby. Remember, the one I told you—"

"I remember." Feeling cross, she pulled the carrier back out of the car and propped it between her hip and the open car door while she tried coaxing Chandler to take the pacifier. At last he did, his cries ceasing as his lips worked rhythmically.

"He's hungry."

"I'm aware of that." And her breasts positively ached for relief. But she wasn't going to tell this man *that.* Not that she needed to, she realized with a hot flush, because his eyes had definitely been eyeing her there. "Don't you have planes to fly somewhere or something?"

His eyes crinkled and he gently, firmly, nudged her out of the way, easily replacing her hands on the carrier with his own. "I am a pilot," he said as he leaned into the car. "But unfortunately the business end of things keeps me on the ground pretty much these days. There. All set.''

He straightened and Emma could see the carrier had been transformed into a secure car seat. Naturally. She felt like bawling. ''I... Thank you.''

''You're welcome.'' He looked at her, not smiling, just being male and competent and calmly accepting the tears collecting in her eyes. This last made the urge to cry magically fade. ''I'll follow you home.''

His statement was oddly appealing. And as such, completely out of the question. She blinked, moved away from him and his hypnotic scent, and pushed the door closed. He either had to move or have his hip banged.

''What for? To see if I can release the carrier once I get there?'' She knew she was being rude. He had helped her with the carrier, after all. But criminy, the man seemed incapable of taking no for an answer. ''I don't know how to get it through to you, Mr. Montgomery, but you cannot buy me into playing your pretend-marriage game.''

His eyebrows peaked. ''Buy?''

''So please just go make your offer to some other woman.'' *Some other woman who can think straight when you look at her with those green eyes.*

''Buy?'' he repeated.

Emma propped a steadying hand on the car, her attention veering from Chandler to Kyle and back again. Chandler, for the moment, seemed satisfied with his pacifier.

''Yes. Buy.'' Did she have a For Sale sign tattooed on her forehead that was visible only to men or something? ''I'm no actress, Mr. Montgomery, and my mama always told me that anyone with eyesight could see in my face when I was telling a lie. Frankly I can't imagine what you could pay that would make attempting such a pretense *worth my while*. I'd be lying not only for your business deal but also to my friends here. So please, take your…offer to someone else.''

She jingled her car keys. Decided she wasn't finished. ''Better yet, Mr. Montgomery, make your business deal with this other man without lying at all. Don't you think a man who has such staunch values as you've described would prefer a man of integrity to a man who'd resort to a ruse to get his way? Just tell him how the whole misunderstanding began with his stepdaughter.''

Kyle shook his head. ''My integrity is intact, thanks,'' he said shortly. ''And you are making too much of a simple thing, Emma. If the pretense bothers you so greatly, I guess I'm willing to make it a legal reality. An annulment after the merger is complete and our lives will continue on as if nothing had ever happened.''

''Oh, sugar, that's even more ridiculous. I'm a complete stranger to you, but you're willing to marry me to pull off some business deal. Yet you're not willing to tell some man you don't really have a wife, after all? Have you listened to yourself? Do you know how insane that sounds?'' Frankly, she thought, a woman would have to be dead to continue on as if nothing had ever happened after meeting Kyle Montgomery. And she was as insane as he was to be debating the merits of such a ridiculous scheme with him.

"I know exactly what I'm proposing, Emma. I haven't gotten to where I am in life by making foolish choices. Choosing you to be my wife, pretend or otherwise, may be a calculated risk, but it's not remotely insane."

Emma just shook her head and slowly walked around the car to the driver's side, using the car as a support to lean on as she moved. She pulled open the door, then looked at him over the roof. "It's a lovely summer afternoon, Mr. Montgomery. Take a walk in the park over there between the buildings. The flowers are beautiful this time of year. Or go across the street to the diner and tell Millie that you'd like a piece of her indescribably delicious blueberry pie. Tell her I sent you and that it's on me, even. But please, please, give up this ridiculous plan of yours. I can't be a part of it."

"You *refuse* to be, you mean."

"Is there any difference?" She squinted into the sunlight. "My integrity isn't for sale."

"If I thought it was, Emma, I wouldn't have decided you were exactly the person I needed to help me." He stepped closer to the car, pinning her with his intense gaze. "When I said I'd make it worth your while, I merely meant that I wouldn't expect you to give up the next six weeks or so of your life without some recompense. I was thinking more on the order of covering your medical costs for the baby. Establishing a trust for Chandler's future. Providing medical insurance for you and your son for the next several years, at least until you can obtain your music-education degree and become established in your career."

Her lips parted. "How did you know—"

"I know a great deal."

She closed her mouth. All a person had to do was go into the diner a few times and he could learn all the gossip he wanted about the waitresses and regular customers. Most everybody who went into the diner knew what her field of study was and how long she'd been inching toward her degree. She didn't need to start conjuring up silly notions of investigations and dossiers. Just because that was what Jeremy's family had—

She closed off the thought. She wanted to go home and get off her feet for a while, feed her son, hold him close and pretend that her body didn't ache as if it had been twisted inside out.

"Goodbye, Mr. Montgomery. It's been…interesting meeting you." She slid into the car, catching her breath at the sharp "discomfort" of the sudden movement.

As she backed out of her parking spot and drove away, she could see Kyle in her rearview mirror. His hands were pushed in his pockets, his stance relaxed. The afternoon breeze ruffled his chestnut hair.

She pulled up at a stop sign, waiting for the traffic to clear, and looked over at her son. "That man is more trouble than anyone I've ever met."

Chandler blinked his round eyes and sucked enthusiastically at his pacifier. Emma was certain he was agreeing with her.

Emma's apartment was a simple studio over the detached garage behind a big old house owned by Penny Holloman. As soon as she pulled up beside the garage and climbed out of the car, she heard Penny call from the back porch. She watched as the older woman skipped down the porch steps and started across the expansive yard.

Emma smiled with real pleasure and waved at her landlady. She reached in and unstrapped Chandler from the carrier, deciding just to leave it where it was, and carefully lifted his warm little body out just as Penny reached her side.

"Oh, sweetie, he's just a peach." Penny brushed her hands down her colorful shirt before reaching out. "Let me take him. You must be exhausted. I swear, when I had Elliot, they kept me in the hospital for a week. Was I ever glad, let me tell you. The last thing I wanted to do was get back home and start cooking three meals a day when I was a nervous wreck about doing something wrong with a new baby."

Emma's arms felt empty when Penny took Chandler into her own. But the other woman was oohing and ahhing over him, obviously delighted to hold him. Emma collected the plastic bag and her case and drew in a breath as she faced the wooden steps leading up the side of the garage to her apartment.

"I just got home myself, and I'm so sorry I wasn't able to meet you at the hospital," Penny chattered on, taking Emma's overnighter from her. "You shouldn't be carrying that," she chastised, heading up the stairs. "If I could have canceled my meeting, I would have. I feel terrible that you drove yourself home like this."

"Don't worry about it," Emma followed her landlady more slowly. Once she got Chandler fed and settled, she was definitely going to take a few of those extra-strength pain relievers her doctor had advised. "Megan agreed to, but I said no. We were fine." She made it to the landing and pushed open the door, stopping short. "Oh, my!"

Penny laughed and rested her cheek on Chandler's head. "Isn't it fabulous? Why didn't you tell me you'd met a man? Because I know for certain that good-for-nothing Jeremy St. James would never have been so extravagant."

Emma cautiously stepped into her apartment. Glorious displays of summer flowers decorated every single surface. An enormous bouquet of yellow and white balloons hovered above her small round dining table. "I haven't met a man," she murmured faintly. Cheerful daisies graced the small table just inside the door and she touched one of the blooms. "Well, nobody except... No. He wouldn't have. He couldn't—"

"Who? Kyle Montgomery perhaps? He is a handsome one. And quite determined, too."

Emma felt light-headed. She dumped the plastic bag on the floor and cautiously lowered herself to the couch. "Kyle...was here?"

"Earlier today." Penny nodded. She flipped open a changing pad on top of the table and gently settled Chandler on top of it. In seconds she'd changed his diaper and carried him back to Emma. "There you go, sweetie. You feed him and I'll get some lunch started for you."

Emma had a lot of questions, but her son's hunger was the primary need. She opened her blouse and situated her son in her arms. He latched on greedily and she chuckled and winced both at once. "Good thing you know what you're doing there, pumpkin, 'cause if it was up to me, I'd still be fumbling around."

Penny must have heard her, because she laughed lightly. "When Elliot was born, bottle feeding was the preferred choice. Herman was horrified when I insisted on nursing our baby." She came back into the room, carrying a tray with a sandwich, a cup of soup and a tall glass of lemonade, which she set on the metal footlocker Emma used as a coffee table. She nudged it within reach of Emma, then pushed the footrest she'd given Emma for Christmas the year before next to the couch.

Emma lifted her feet onto it and let out a long relieved breath. But Penny wasn't finished. Not until she'd taken Emma's two bed pillows from the top shelf in the closet where they were kept during the day and propped them behind Emma's neck and under her knees.

"There. That's better, isn't it?" Penny patted her hand and continued moving around the small apartment, unpacking the few items from Emma's overnighter and adding the baby items from the plastic bag to the secondhand chest of drawers Emma had found. "Too bad your mother can't be here to help you," Penny said.

Emma shook her head. That was the last thing she needed. "Mama's helping my sisters back home with the grandkids she already has." She shifted against the pillows and sighed sleepily. "She doesn't understand why I'm a single mother, anyway, so her helping would have been accompanied by a lot of lectures I don't want to hear. Once a week is plenty for me.''

''The only one needing a good lecture is that pimple on the face of society who left you to fend for yourself.''

Emma managed to smile at the caustic description of Jeremy St. James.

''Fortunately I'm able to wholeheartedly say that I approve of your new choice,'' Penny went on.

''If you're referring to Kyle Montgomery, he is *not* my new choice. He's just...''

Penny waited expectantly, her eyes sparkling with expectation. ''Just handsome enough to make even my old bones sit up and take notice?''

''You're not old.''

Penny chuckled. ''Old enough to know a perfect match when I see one. A grown man doesn't track down a landlady at a church committee meeting to gain access to his young lady's apartment where he proceeds to fill it with every flower known to humankind if he's not totally smitten.''

Totally determined, totally insane and totally off-limits. ''I don't even know the man,'' Emma insisted. ''I met him just this morning.''

A fact that seemed to delight Penny even more. ''Well, you certainly made an impression on him,'' she said. ''I'll leave you to rest now, but I'll come back this evening with some supper for you.''

''You don't have to do that, Penny. I can manage.''

Penny stopped at the door and shook her head. ''I know you can manage, sweetie. But sometimes you don't have to do it *all* on your own, so let me help in the ways that I can.'' She plucked a small white envelope out of the daisy arrangement and handed it to Emma. ''Your admirer left this for you.'' She winked and went out the door, shutting only the outer screen. Emma heard her footsteps on the stairway, then all was quiet again, except for the thumping of her pulse in her ears.

She nibbled the inside of her lip, turning the small envelope over in her fingers. He had nothing to say that she wanted to hear. Or, in this case, *read*.

''Oh, Emma, honestly. It's just a card.'' She tore open the envelope and pulled out the flat card.

Chandler is blessed to have such a lovely mother.

Emma's eyes blurred. She looked down at her son to find him looking up at her. ''We're both blessed, aren't we, pumpkin? I just figured that a man like Kyle Montgomery wouldn't be able to see that.''

She lifted Chandler to her shoulder and readjusted her clothes. Kissing his cheek, she brought her legs up onto the couch and lay back, cradling him securely.

Then she closed her eyes and they both slept.

Chapter Three

By the next morning Emma decided she owed her mother an apology. Hattie Valentine had had six daughters, managing to feed and clothe them all, for the most part single-handedly.

Emma, however, seemed to be completely out of her element with just one baby. Chandler wanted to eat every other hour, which meant she got very little sleep. Sometime in the middle of the night she gave up on the notion of having the baby sleep in his bassinet and just kept him in bed with her. She stacked diapers and wipes on the floor beside them and slept when he slept. Fed him when hungry, changed him when wet.

This was not at all the way it was supposed to go, according to her *Now You Are a Mother!* book which spouted tripe about four-hour schedules and other such nonsense.

By midmorning, her small home looked like a tornado had torn through it, leaving flowers and minute baby T-shirts and receiving blankets behind.

Penny came by, took in the chaos without a blink of surprise and shooed Emma into the bathroom where, she assured her, she'd feel better after a nice long shower.

"As soon as I'm under the water, he'll be hungry," Emma had protested tiredly. "I'll shower…oh, I don't know, when he's two years old."

Penny had laughed and scooped Chandler off Emma's lap. "I think I hear a verse of the baby blues somewhere in there." She'd waved toward the bathroom. "Go on now. You need a few minutes for yourself."

Emma wasn't so sure, but she'd gone. She looked at herself in the mirror, grimaced and turned on the shower. A half hour later she emerged to find her apartment tidied up, Chandler sleeping and Penny nowhere in sight.

"Sure," she whispered lovingly over Chandler in the bassinet. "*Now* you sleep."

A creak on the stairs outside told her someone was coming up. Probably Penny. Emma adjusted the strap of her red sundress and smoothed back her wet hair. "You were right," she said as she went to the wood-framed screen door and pushed it open. "I do feel better."

"My sisters always say that flowers make a woman feel better," Kyle Montgomery said smoothly as he reached the top step and smiled at her. He looked dismayingly appealing in pleated khakis, a whiter-than-white collarless shirt and navy jacket. Laugh lines fanned out from his eyes. "Your landlady said you were up and about. You look very nice in red. Fresh as a wild poppy."

Emma flushed. Her hair hung straight and wet to her shoulders, her feet were bare, and the poppy-red dress stretched too tightly across her chest. She crossed her arms and moistened her lips. "Thank you for the flowers and card. It was very nice."

A smile flirted with his lips as he looked at her. "May I come in?"

Emma swallowed. "I'm not sure that's a good idea."

"Why not?"

"Because I'll probably end up being rude to you, and being surrounded by beautiful flowers from you when that happens seems like it'd be in poor taste."

"Rude? Ah, Emma, I think you've just been honest. I'm glad you like the flowers, though. I have one sister who insists roses are the only flower worth receiving, but you didn't seem like the rose type to me."

"I'm allergic to them," Emma said shortly. The last man to give her roses had thoroughly betrayed her. She wasn't sure she'd ever disassociate roses from that awful time.

Kyle's eyebrow peaked. "How fortunate I chose otherwise, then." He reached past her through the doorway to the daisies sitting just inside and snapped off a bloom. He lifted his hand, frowning slightly when Emma gave a startled jump.

She clenched her teeth, flushing again when he

tucked the short stem of the daisy behind her ear. She swallowed and stepped away from the door, silently allowing him entry.

He walked to the center of the living area, seeming to dominate the space. "How's Chandler?"

Emma shut the screen quietly. "Fine. Sleeping at the moment."

He nodded, glanced at the blank wall opposite the couch. "Why did you get rid of the piano?"

Emma frowned. "How do you know I had a piano?"

He walked over to the spot where her upright had stood for three years. He brushed a leather boot over the permanent indentations the heavy instrument had made in her taupe-colored carpet. "I noticed the marks on the rug earlier. Why, Emma?"

She shrugged. "I'm sure you've already come to your own conclusion."

"You needed the money."

"I had other payments that were more important," she corrected.

"How long have you played?"

"The piano?" *Not long enough.* "Since I was thirteen." She'd been caught sneaking into the church back in Dooley, Tennessee. But instead of hauling her back to her mother with a few strong words, Reverend Harold Chandler had decided Emma could use the piano twice a week in the afternoons after school. They couldn't afford lessons, but Emma had used the music books at the church, and by the time she'd graduated from high school, she'd taught herself enough to earn a modest music scholarship.

She owed a lot to Reverend Chandler.

"I envy you," he said.

She lifted her eyebrows. "Whatever for?"

He shrugged. "I took piano lessons when I was sixteen. Never did get the hang of it. I could play the notes, I guess. Just not…the *music*."

Oh, she really didn't want to hear anything like that from this man. It bespoke a sensitivity in him she didn't want to acknowledge. It was easier, safer, casting him as the rich man intent on doing a business deal no matter what.

After all, it wasn't as if her one foray into the man-woman arena had been a terrific success. Her judgment had been faulty, her sensibility nonexistent.

Emma nibbled the inside of her lip and sat down on the couch. "Isn't it a workday, Kyle? Shouldn't you be out running your business rather than discussing the finer aspects of being a musician?"

"That's what I like about you, Emma. You get right to the point."

"Which is?"

He sat down on the other end of the couch and stretched his arm along the back. His jacket gaped, exposing more of the shirt he wore beneath.

Emma turned her eyes from the sight of his strong brown throat rising from the open collar.

"This is business for me, Emma. You know that." He looked toward the bassinet situated near the table, presenting Emma with his profile.

It was as perfect as the rest of him. All sharp angles and utterly masculine.

"I was invited to Payton Cummings's dinner party on Sunday evening. I've told him I can't join them because I've other commitments. Family commitments. I'd prefer to back up that statement with some semblance of truth.''

His fingertips were inches from her shoulder and she shifted, putting more distance between them. ''You've said you have sisters. Make plans with them. It's less of a lie than using Chandler and me.''

Kyle shook his head. ''Tell me what you need in life, Emma Valentine, and I'll do my damnedest to make it so, if you'll just help me with this. Forget about this *buying* notion you've got in your head and look at it as one favor for another.''

''I need my son,'' she said, exasperated, ''but I need no favors from you or any other man.'' She pushed to her feet, pacing to the bassinet and back again.

''He really did a number on you, didn't he?'' Kyle's gaze followed her. ''The jerk who was stupid enough to leave you alone and pregnant.''

''You know nothing about it.''

He nodded thoughtfully. ''No, I don't. It's your business entirely. But I can protect you from him.''

Emma swallowed. Little did he know she didn't need protection from anyone, least of all the St. James family. They wanted nothing to do with her. Had ensured it. And she didn't need Kyle Montgomery coming in here, smelling like a dream, reminding her how foolish she'd been.

Kyle rose and stepped close to her, bringing with him his addictive scent. He touched her chin with his finger. ''I can protect Chandler.''

There was no wheedling in his voice. Only the simple utterly confident assurance of a man who'd been around long enough to know his abilities. One who'd been around enough to pinpoint the one thing that would penetrate her defenses.

"Come on, Emma. Help me."

She hesitated. He was so close she could see the darker rim of green around his irises. "Kyle, I—"

"Yoo-hoo, anybody up there?" Footsteps pounded up the stairs outside and Emma blinked, stepping back. She cleared her throat and crossed to the screen door, looking out to see Millie Johnson, her boss at the diner, coming up. "I've brought food," she said when she saw Emma. She lifted the cardboard box that was filled to the brim with foam containers and foil-wrapped packages. "It'll last you a few days, and then I'll replace it with more while I try to talk you into taking more than two weeks off with the baby. You need six weeks, and that's that."

Emma just shook her head. Her boss, her friend, had a heart wider than the Colorado sky. "Come on in, Millie. I'm not sure where I'll put the food, though. Penny's been keeping the fridge stocked, too." She smiled wryly. "Apparently my friends think I'm in danger of starving to death on my own."

"Oh, shush." Millie brushed past her, stopping in surprise at the sight of a man inside. She recovered quickly, though, introducing herself as she strode across to the small kitchen.

Kyle raked his fingers through his hair, squelching an impatient sigh at this latest interruption. He'd been reaching her, dammit. He knew it. He'd seen it in her chocolate-brown eyes. He slid a business card from the inner pocket on his jacket and handed it to Emma. "I can be reached anytime, anywhere, at that number," he said softly. "But I need an answer soon."

She hesitated, obviously indecisive. But then she reached for the card, her slender fingers carefully avoiding his longer darker ones as she took it from him. "I gave you my answer yesterday."

"Think about it," Kyle suggested. "I'll be in touch if I don't hear from you."

"A threat?"

Her sarcasm didn't faze him. "I have no reason to threaten you, Emma. We can be on the same side. You're completely safe from me." He was making the promise to her as much as to himself, he realized. When she looked up at him with her wide wary eyes, he was reminded of fairy-tale heroines.

Disgusted with the direction of his thoughts, he strode to the door. He'd given up on fairy tales when he was seven. "I'll look forward to hearing from you, Emma." He left then, carrying the image of her studying his card with a sober expression on her lovely unadorned face.

After Millie's brief visit, Emma fixed some lunch for herself and freshened the water for the flowers. Then Chandler awakened and she gathered her courage to give him his first bath. It was a rousing success, and as soon as she finished slipping his wriggling little arms and legs into his lightweight romper, he sighed with his whole little self and went to sleep, perfect as an angel.

Emma sat watching him for long minutes, nearly sitting on her hands to keep from touching him, from disturbing him simply because she wanted to feel his warmth. "My little man," she whispered, then began humming under her breath. Her fingers automatically moved with the music that was vivid and brilliant in her mind, and realizing it, she clasped them in her lap.

It wasn't as if she'd never play again, she reasoned. Every week when she worked with the children's choir at the Benderhoff school, she'd be playing piano. But it wasn't the same as sitting at her own instrument whenever she wanted, playing to her heart's content.

"I'll teach you to play," she promised Chandler softly. Then she frowned as Kyle's words whispered through her mind. He'd learned the notes, but he'd known the true heart of the music wasn't there for him. "You'll feel the music, too, pumpkin. Whether it's piano or something else, we'll share that joy. I know it."

The afternoon was passing when she again heard feet on the steps outside. This time, however, she was expecting visitors, and she went to the door, smiling at the two women coming up. She'd met Taylor Fletcher and Megan Malone at the Buttonwood Baby Clinic when they'd all been taking the same childbirth classes. Except Megan was Megan Macgregor now, thoroughly adored by her new husband, Mac.

Megan had her baby, Tyler, in her arms and led the way up the stairs, while Taylor, enormously pregnant, followed more slowly.

Once they reached the top, Emma held open the door. "We should have met at the diner or something, Taylor. I just didn't think about you having to climb the stairs."

Taylor rolled her eyes and awkwardly settled on

the couch, folding her arms across her belly. "Which is worse?" she asked breathlessly. "Me climbing stairs at this stage or you climbing stairs immediately after having a baby?" She looked over at the bassinet. "But you can bring Master Valentine over to see me, if you don't mind, because I think I'm stuck here on the couch for the duration."

Megan settled on the couch, too, resting Tyler on her lap. "Yup. Bring him over here, Emma. Let's compare birthing horror stories and scare Taylor silly."

Taylor snorted softly and Emma shook her head at the two women. She rolled the bassinet toward them, trying to jostle it as little as possible. Then she handed out glasses of lemonade and set a tray of cookies from one of the foil packages of Millie's on the metal footlocker and sat down to catch up with her friends.

"So what's with the floral display?" Taylor finally asked when all the gossip was expended. "It looks like you received flowers from every customer who has ever gone into Mom & Pop's."

"Kyle Montgomery," Emma answered without thinking.

Megan's eyebrows shot up. "As in Kyle Montgomery, head of ChandlerAIR? I read an article recently about him. He's—"

"I know." Emma folded her arms over the edge of the bassinet and gently smoothed Chandler's hair.

"How did you meet him? I thought you were totally off men after what Jeremy St. James did." Taylor tried to sit forward to reach the cookies, but couldn't. Emma leaned over and handed her two.

"I am not *off* men," Emma defended. "I just don't need or want one, that's all."

"Famous last words," Megan quipped.

"Besides," Emma continued, ignoring Megan's comment, "he's not interested in me. Well, not *that* way."

"Oh, now this is sounding *really* interesting," Taylor said lightly. "Come on, Emma, tell me. Then I can live vicariously on the excitement in your life."

"I wouldn't call it exciting to have yet another man try to buy me off."

Both her friends' faces sobered.

"Oh, that's not exactly right," Emma admitted, feeling frustration well up all over again. "He visited me yesterday morning with the most outrageous proposition." She told them the bare bones of Kyle's suggestion. "I told him no, of course."

"No!" Megan stared at her, dismayed. "But Emma, think of what a man like Kyle Montgomery can offer in return for your help."

Taylor was nodding, too.

"It doesn't matter," Emma insisted. "I'll manage just fine with Chandler."

"How?" Taylor asked bluntly. "By selling your television set next? By taking on a *third* job? Emma, you're barely scraping by, and only a week ago you told me your latest fantasy was buying health insurance."

She'd expected her friends' support. She stood up and began pacing. Among the flowers, she fancied that the memory of Kyle's aftershave still lingered. "He's just another rich man thinking he can buy his way through life. I don't want any part of it. It's dishonest.''

Megan rose too, cradling her baby in one arm and catching Emma's hand with her other. "Emma, I know how hard this must be for you. But Chandler is *here*. You have to think about him. What's best for him. Maybe taking this offer is something you should seriously consider.''

Emma looked away from her friend's warm hazel eyes. "You agree with her, don't you, Taylor?''

The younger woman nodded. "That's what a good mother does," she murmured. "Thinks of her child first.''

Emma felt her eyes burn. Taylor had already decided to give up her child for adoption to a family who could provide for her baby in a way she herself couldn't. She was younger than both Megan and Emma, yet Emma felt that Taylor was quite possibly the bravest woman she'd ever met.

She dashed her hands across her eyes, then propped them on her hips, sniffing hugely. "Shootfire," she said in her best Southern drawl. "This afternoon wasn't supposed to be a weepy wallow. I've told the man no, so that's all there is to it. He's probably findin' himself another young bride as we speak." Then she focused on Megan. "And speaking of brides, how is married life treating *you*, Mrs. Macgregor?''

Megan smiled and said that married life was terrific, but her gaze met Emma's meaningfully. Fortunately, however, she didn't return to the subject of Kyle, and soon Taylor asked Emma if the labor and delivery was really just a matter of "discomfort" as the leaders of the childbirth class kept telling them.

Emma snorted and Megan laughed. Taylor blew out a huge breath and moaned. "That's what I was afraid of." She struggled to her feet to go to the bathroom.

"You're still planning to return to work next week?" Megan asked Emma.

"To Benderhoff," Emma said. "Their summer session begins and I'll be teaching two afternoon classes there." She'd always enjoyed the classes she taught part-time at the private school. But she was willing to teach this session specifically for the money it would bring. Money that would eventually pay the hospital bill. "Millie says that if I set foot in the diner before two weeks are up, she'll shoot me with that shotgun she keeps in the back. If she had her way, I'd take off three times that long."

"What about your fall semester?" Megan asked quietly. "How can you fit in your own classes?"

Emma swallowed, then managed a bright smile she knew didn't fool her friend. "I'm going to take off next semester. It'll be a nice break." She just hoped the one semester didn't stretch into two. Or three. She'd already spent so long working toward her degree that every delay was frustrating. Even this one.

Taylor came out then, pressing her hands to her back. Emma hugged her friends, thanked them for the baby outfits they'd brought for Chandler and watched them carefully descend the steps before climbing into Megan's vehicle.

She stood on the landing for a few minutes,

breathing in the crisp clear air. Someone was barbecuing nearby. She could smell the distinctive delectable scent of sizzling steak. A dog barked, and someone was mowing a lawn.

It was a beautiful summer evening. She had her health and a perfect child. There was no reason to feel the panic welling in her chest. No reason at all.

She went inside and picked up Chandler, rocking him in her arms as she paced her small living room. She didn't look at Kyle's card, which she'd left on the dining table. But she was painfully aware of it sitting there between a bouquet of bright orange daylilies and a yellow balloon that had lost some of its helium and was hovering an inch over the table.

"I love you, pumpkin. I'll never let you down," she pledged, pressing her lips to Chandler's head. He wriggled and Emma chuckled. "Always hungry. Well, food is something I seem to have lots of for you."

Kyle called at precisely seven that evening. Emma's answer hadn't changed, but she was grateful he hadn't shown up in person this time. It was difficult enough reiterating her "no" over an impersonal telephone line.

He didn't sound unduly disturbed by their brief exchange, which made Emma think even more strongly that he probably had several other women waiting as backups. Kyle Montgomery was the kind of man who had best-case scenarios and worst-case scenarios planned to the nth detail.

While Chandler slept, Emma wrote thank-you notes for the various gifts and cards she'd received,

then set about looking through the pile of mail she'd
been receiving and ignoring for the past week.

There was a long chatty letter from her mother.
All about Emma's sisters—*married* sisters, that
was—Emma's nieces and nephews, and Hattie's job
at the grocery store in Dooley. There were cards from
two of her regular customers at Millie's and a letter
from Benderhoff. Emma slit it open, expecting a note
about the baby or about the upcoming session.

What she wasn't expecting was the polite missive
saying that her services wouldn't be required, after
all. She didn't even rate a thank-you for the past two
years.

She read it through twice, sure she'd misunderstood. She'd been teaching at Benderhoff steadily.
Her work had always been more than satisfactory, or
so she'd been told at each review period. Telling herself not to panic, she went into the kitchen and
yanked out her telephone directory. She found the
home number of Emil Craddock, the headmaster of
Benderhoff and dialed it with a shaking finger. They
wouldn't do this to her. They couldn't.

But five minutes later she hung up again, knowing
that they *had*. She paced. She added numbers in her
head. She thought of ways she could get by without
the money—the rather good money—she'd earned at
Benderhoff.

She finally pulled out her sofa bed, lay down with
Chandler beside her and tried to make herself sleep
while he slept. But sleep didn't come. All she could
remember was growing up in Dooley, getting her
clothing secondhand from the rummage sales at
church, doing the grocery shopping with her two

older sisters, following their mama's list to the letter because they had to pay with food stamps and only certain things were eligible.

At four o'clock in the morning Emma finally climbed out of bed and retrieved the business card from the table. She turned on the light in the kitchen and, heedless of the hour, reached for the phone, dialing hurriedly, before she lost her nerve. It rang only twice. Then Kyle's voice, husky and deep, answered.

She swallowed, but the enormous knot in her throat didn't go away. "Is your offer still on the table?"

"You know it is, Emma."

She drew in a short breath. "Then I accept. I'll pretend to be your wife until your business deal goes through."

"I'll be at your place in a couple of hours."

A tear leaked from the corner of her tightly closed eyes. She was grateful that he didn't express any undue pleasure or satisfaction. That his voice was as steady and sure as ever. "We'll be ready," she said.

Then she hung up and went to pack her clothes and Chandler's stretchy little sleepers and diapers. They were the easy things.

She couldn't help thinking, though, that she was also packing away her honesty. And that wasn't easy at all.

Chapter Four·

"This is everything?"

Emma rubbed her hand over Chandler's back. She focused on the suitcases she'd left sitting in the center of her apartment. Kyle was picking them up with ease. "For now," she replied.

He glanced over his shoulder at her, one eyebrow raised. "If there's more, we might as well take them."

"It's just winter clothes and things that won't fit Chandler for months yet." By then, Kyle's need for a wife would be past and she and her son would be back home. Her life would return to normal, and all that would remain to remind her of this time would be the knowledge that she'd had a price, after all.

"If you're sure."

She nodded, even though she wasn't sure of anything, particularly with Kyle standing there with her discount-store suitcases tucked under his arms. They surely did clash with his Rolex watch, she thought.

Chandler squirmed and made a noise, and she pressed her lips to his head, cradling him closely. She stepped out of the way so that Kyle could go out the doorway, then she followed him, picking up Chandler's diaper bag.

"Leave it," Kyle said. "I'll come back for it."

The bag was stuffed to the gills with diapers and wipes and powder and lotion. It shouldn't have weighed a ton, but it felt as if it did. She reluctantly left it sitting on the end table by the daisies and carefully descended the stairs. Kyle had stored the suitcases in the trunk and was waiting by the open passenger door.

Emma looked from his sleek black car to her sturdy orange sedan—ancient and built like a tank. "I should follow you. Then I'll have my car and—"

"It would be better if you left your car here," he said smoothly. "I've got a second vehicle at home that you can use to your heart's content."

Her stomach clenched uncomfortably, and she kept the rest of her suggestion to herself: that she could fit Chandler's bassinet easily into her back seat. He probably figured her old car was too much of an eyesore for the rarefied atmosphere of his neighborhood.

Well, Emma Valentine, you've made your bed... She could almost hear her mother's voice.

"I've already moved Chandler's seat into the back seat of my car. Can you get him into it, or would you like me to?"

"I will." She didn't look at him as he placed his hand on the top of the open door, waiting. But she couldn't help noticing the sprinkling of dark hair on burnished skin, taut tendons and strong, well-groomed hands.

Reaching into the narrow rear of his car was awkward, but she managed to get Chandler into the seat and fasten the harness. He slept through the whole process, but Emma felt positively out of breath by the time she straightened.

Kyle caught her elbow when she swayed. "You okay?"

She nodded and slid herself into the passenger side. A sinfully soft leather seat cradled her like loving arms. She gathered in the trailing hem of her ankle-length broomstick skirt, and Kyle pushed the door closed before heading up the steps again. She heard the slap of her wooden screen door and in moments he reappeared with the diaper bag.

He strode around to the driver's side and set the bag in the back next to Chandler, then slid behind the wheel with an ease Emma couldn't help but envy.

The engine came to life with a low throaty growl, and he backed away from the garage, her apartment, her car and her hold on reality.

She bit her lip, turning her eyes away from the sight. It was a gray dawn, and Penny's house was still dark. She hadn't even told her what she was doing. She'd have to call her. Make some type of explanation.

Kyle shifted gears, and when his hand inadvertently brushed her thigh, Emma jerked. He glanced

at her without comment as he drove out of the alley
onto the morning-quiet street.

Emma swallowed, the silence in the car weighing
her down. She stared out the side window as they
passed the diner and headed east. She wasn't surprised. Naturally a man like Kyle would have his
home in the wealthier section of town. Eastridge.
She'd once had hazy dreams of living in one of the
sparkling new homes with a three-car garage and a
pool out back. Living in one of the homes as Jeremy's wife.

They drove through the exclusive area. Passed the
discreet sign that directed individuals to the outstand-
ing Benderhoff facility. She stifled a sigh and looked
over her shoulder at Chandler.

"We'll be there in a few minutes," Kyle said.

Emma nodded, and surreptitiously rubbed her
palms down her thighs.

"Baxter will probably have breakfast waiting. I've
got to go to the airport for a while. A few hours. But
then I'll come home and we can do some shopping."

Who was Baxter? "Shopping?"

"For the nursery. I had a decorator in for most of
the house." He turned down an unmarked road, taking them into the rising sun.

Emma looked out the back window at the residen-
tial area they'd left behind.

"Something wrong?"

"No. I…well, I assumed you lived in Eastridge,"
she admitted.

He shook his head and kept driving. And Emma,
who had lived in Buttonwood for several years, realized she didn't have a clue where they were. The

paved road, only wide enough to accommodate two passing cars, curved and climbed. Then they rounded a sharp outcropping of rocks and shot down again, straight toward a spectacular house that seemed an actual part of the ridge that overlooked Buttonwood.

Kyle pulled up into a drive that was narrow simply because two-thirds of it was being excavated. He parked in front of the house before turning to look at Emma. He hoped she liked it. Only because he wanted her to be comfortable here, he rapidly assured himself. But she was facing out the side window and he couldn't see her reaction, except for the fingertips she drummed silently against her thigh, which was draped with her purple-and-pink skirt. "I realize it's not Eastridge, but do you think it'll do?"

Her fingers went still and she looked at him. "It's big." Then her eyes widened slightly and her cheeks colored. "And…lovely."

He smiled faintly. "Did you expect a circus tent or something?"

"No. No, of course not." Her lips pressed together for a moment. "Who is Baxter?"

"Baxter?" Kyle looked beyond Emma toward the house. How to describe the man. His conscience? His friend? "My housekeeper," he said after a moment. "But he'd say butler. He'll be crazy about Chandler. You'll probably see more of him than me, actually."

Which didn't seem to reassure her any, Kyle thought, noticing the way her fingers started drumming again. "I'm sure he heard us drive up and is probably setting breakfast on the table as we speak." He climbed out of the car and went around to open her door, helping her from the low-slung vehicle. He should have brought the Land Rover. He'd thought it about a dozen times since he'd parked outside her garage apartment.

This family stuff would take some adjusting.

Before she could contort herself into the narrow space to reach the car seat, Kyle reached past her and handed her the diaper bag, then scooped out the baby. He straightened, automatically situating the baby in one arm. Then he closed Emma's car door and settled his free hand at the small of her back, his fingertips tingling at the contact with her soft shirt.

He focused on the white-haired man who'd opened the front door and waited on the porch. Kyle didn't need to look at Baxter's disapproving gaze to know the man didn't like what he, Kyle, was doing. Not with the pretend-family bit, and certainly not with his determination to acquire CCS.

Ignoring Baxter for the moment, he slid the diaper bag from Emma's shoulder and touched her back again, which earned him another wide-eyed look. "Relax. We're not gonna stuff you in an oven and eat you."

"I am relaxed."

He raised a brow, disbelieving. "Let's go inside." He nudged her forward along the narrow stone walkway. It was scheduled to be widened and graded within the next few weeks.

"Bax, this is Emma Valentine and Chandler. Emma, Baxter. Anything you need, he's the man." Kyle eyed him as they approached.

Baxter turned up his nose at Kyle and focused, instead, on the baby in his arms. "There's a handsome boy, with a good solid name. May I?" He lifted

Chandler away from Kyle at Emma's nod. He brought his wrinkled aristocratic-looking face close to the baby and cooed.

Kyle caught Emma's eye. "Told you so," he murmured.

"Breakfast is on the patio, sir. Miss Emma." Baxter turned and headed back into the house, still cooing to the baby.

"Does he have grandchildren?"

Kyle shook his head. "No family." Except him. "I think the man was a nanny in a past life, though. Bax, who won't start the day without a starched shirt, tie and crisp black suit, sees a person under two feet tall and goes into coochy-coo mode." The housekeeper also made no bones about his belief that Kyle was throwing away the best years of his life by concentrating so exclusively on his business.

Emma smiled, but she was obviously uneasy. He could see it in her eyes, as well as the arms she'd crossed tightly across her chest.

"If you don't want Bax to take the baby, you can tell him so," Kyle said. "He'll understand."

She uncrossed her arms, only to twist her fingers together. "No, it's okay."

"For a few minutes, anyway," he guessed.

She smiled, a little more easily. "For a few minutes."

"Just like my sister. She didn't want to let her baby out of her sight, either. Come on. Breakfast will be getting cold."

Emma swallowed and stepped into the foyer, then realized her mouth had dropped open and quickly snapped it shut.

The interior of the house wasn't at all like the exterior.

"What do you think?"

He'd had a decorator, she reminded herself. "The windows are fabulous," she said truthfully. They lined the wall ahead of her, giving a beautiful view of Buttonwood beyond the expansive gardens outside the windows.

"I liked them," Kyle said behind her. "Looking out and seeing sky."

Which didn't seem to fit with the coldly beautiful marble, glass and miles of white furnishings any more than those very furnishings fit the nature-blending exterior of the house.

"You mentioned a nursery?" Lord, she hoped the nursery was an empty undecorated room. She could bring some bright cheerful pillows from home. Pin up a quilt on the wall. Something.

"It's upstairs. But let's eat first."

Emma nibbled the inside of her lip, but nodded. She followed him through the wintry house and breathed a sigh of relief when she stepped through French doors that opened onto the garden.

Out there it truly was lovely. Bushes and riotous flowers and lush green grass. Right in the middle of the garden was a lovely glass and verdigris table with matching chairs. The fresh fruit, juices and covered silver serving dishes set on the table looked like something out of a gourmet magazine. Which, of course, made her stomach rumble.

She pressed her palm to her waist, hoping Kyle hadn't heard the distinctive sound. But she suspected by the deepening corner of his mouth that he had.

He pulled out one of the iron chairs for her, then sat across from her, his back to the sharp drop-off. She realized there was an iron fence hidden amid the thick hedges. Beyond that, Buttonwood spread out like a jewel.

She closed her eyes and breathed in the fresh morning air, the flowers, the *green*. They'd no sooner seated themselves, though, when Baxter appeared with a cushioned straight-back chair he insisted Emma use.

She switched from the iron chair to the new one, which was truly comfortable. Then she forgot about the view and the chairs because Kyle sat across from her. Impossibly compelling. Indolent and urbane. Smooth and quietly powerful.

He unsettled her. Pure and simple.

So she focused on Baxter, who'd replaced his severe black suit coat for a baby sling, which held her son cozily against his chest. And Chandler was obviously content as a snug bug, since he slept through the pouring of coffee and juice, the uncovering of a steaming platter of fluffy scrambled eggs and bacon. Baxter asked if she cared for anything else.

"No, thank you, Mr. Baxter. This looks lovely."

He beamed approvingly. "Just Baxter, Miss." He looked at Kyle wordlessly, then returned to the kitchen.

Emma eyed Kyle, but his attention was on the food he was piling onto his plate. The early sunshine glinted off his hair, highlighting deep strands of auburn.

He looked up then, his eyes focusing on her with disturbing intensity. "Emma, stop worrying."

"I wasn't... Yes, I was." And it bothered her that he'd been able to see it. "I can't help it." She picked up her fork, held it suspended over her plate. "My mama says I came out of the womb that way. Worrying."

His eyes crinkled. "And where *is* your mama?"

"Tennessee."

"She's not able to come and see her grandson?"

"Mama's got lots of grandkids." He just kept watching her steadily and Emma found the words coming without volition. "Chandler is just one more, except I didn't have the good grace to get married first like my sisters did."

"She'll feel differently when she holds Chandler in her arms. I can arrange for her to visit if you'd like. The flight would—"

"Mama would never get on an airplane," Emma said hurriedly. Even if Emma had been able to afford the plane ticket for her mother to visit, it would have been wasted. Hattie Valentine traveled by bus or car or not at all. Not even Kyle Montgomery could change that. And her mother definitely wouldn't approve of her middle daughter's latest "shenanigans."

"What about your father?"

"What about him?" She looked straight at him.

He stared right back. "I don't like discussing the man who contributed to my existence, either," he murmured after a moment.

Emma's gaze fell, unable to withstand the intensity in his. Nor the empathy. Then her stomach growled again.

"Eat, Emma."

Cheeks burning, she poked her fork into the eggs and ate.

The nursery, when Kyle eventually led the way upstairs after showing her through the rest of the glacially decorated first floor, was blessedly plain. Emma was also pleased to see that it shared the same panoramic view of the gardens, Buttonwood and the brilliant blue sky. The room had a high ceiling, plain white walls and a warm hardwood floor. Not a piece of marble or chrome in sight.

There was a connecting door to a smaller bedroom beside it, which contained a wide four-poster bed, nightstands and a matching chest of drawers. Emma wanted to sag with relief, but she controlled herself and moved across the squishy carpet to open a closed door. It revealed a spacious walk-in closet.

She looked over at Kyle. His hair seemed darker against the backdrop of the white room. "You kept the decorator from coming upstairs?"

"I can call her back this week if you'd like."

"No!" Emma said hurriedly. "No, I didn't mean that at all. The rooms are just fine the way they are."

"You can pick out what you like for furnishings when we go out later. And whatever you need for the nursery, of course."

"Chandler's bassinet is fine for now," Emma said. "I can bring it over here when I get my car."

"I already said you wouldn't need your car."

"Maybe I want my car. Just because it's not the type of car *your* wife would drive doesn't mean—"

"Hold on there, Emma. The only reason you won't need it is because I've a Land Rover you can use. I don't care if you want to drive a tank or a

Ferrari, as long as it's road worthy. But until the work is finished on the drive, there simply isn't room for three vehicles here.''

She propped her hands on her hips. ''Sugar, I saw the size of the garage off the side of the house. It could handle a fleet of cars.''

''Ordinarily that's true. But right now it's got the skeleton of an old Lockheed P38 in it, and that takes up a sight more room than that gunboat you drive. Give me a chance to reorganize things a little, and you'll have your car here with you. Okay?''

She blinked. Nodded. It certainly wasn't the explanation she'd expected. And she actually felt badly for having misjudged him.

''In any case,'' Kyle went on as if they hadn't had the little sidetrack about cars and garages, ''you'll need more for the nursery than a bassinet. Don't you want a rocking chair and—''

''We're not going to be here all that long, anyway, so there's no point in buying a lot of things.''

''There's every point.'' Kyle straightened from his slouch against the wall. ''As far as everyone else is concerned, you and Chandler belong here. Naturally I'd provide for my family. What new parents don't go out and buy everything on the planet they can afford for their new child, whether it's necessary or not? I learned that quite well when my sister had her baby.''

''For goodness' sake, Kyle. Do you think Mr. Cummings is going to want to snoop around your house to see how well you've equipped your supposed child's nursery?''

''I'm not leaving anything to chance.''

She let out a long breath and closed the closet door. "It's a wonder you didn't find a *real* wife, then," she murmured as she opened the next door. A bathroom. A big beautiful bathroom with a big beautiful bathtub that was practically large enough to swim in. It made her forget for a moment the issue about her car. "Oh, my," she breathed.

"So that's what it takes to impress you," Kyle said, coming up beside her. "A big square whirlpool tub."

"Considering my apartment only has a shower about the size of a postage stamp, you're darned tootin' I appreciate a nice tub." She made a soft sound. "Seems kind of naughty to be discussing showers and tubs with a stranger whose house I'm moving into." And since she'd admitted it, it seemed even more inappropriate.

"Mmm. Naughty." He tugged at his ear, smiling faintly. "There's a word I haven't heard in a while."

Emma felt her cheeks heat. She turned on her heel and walked across the room, out into the wide hall and away from him and his intoxicating scent.

There were several rooms off the hallway, and she wondered which one belonged to Kyle. She hoped it was the one on the end, because it was the farthest away. And seeing how just thinking about Kyle and bedrooms made her feel breathless, she figured distance was a safe thing.

Emma, Emma, Emma. What have you gotten yourself into? She tugged on the hem of her hip-length shirt and headed toward the staircase. The banister was gleaming mahogany and the stairs would have been simply beautiful, like something out of *Gone with the Wind,* if it wasn't for the cold white carpet that flowed over them.

She started down the steps moments before she heard Chandler's demanding cry. Baxter came out of the kitchen, and Emma hurried over to her baby, taking him into her arms with a profound sense of relief. Not that she didn't think Baxter, with his baby sling and all, wasn't quite capable of minding him for a little while. She just preferred to have Chandler with *her.*

"You're hungry aren't you, pumpkin?" She kissed his hand and swayed side to side. She needed to nurse him. Desperately. "I'll just go upstairs now."

Kyle nodded, his eyes on Chandler for a moment. He ran his fingertip over her son's soft cheek, then blinked and stepped back. "Right. I'll be at the office for the next few hours. Bax will help you unpack your things." He strode to the door, scooped up his keys from the table where the diaper bag was and left.

Emma looked at Baxter. "I really can unpack myself," she said in the awkward wake of Kyle's abrupt departure.

"It's no trouble, miss. That's what I'm here for."

"Emma." She moistened her lips. "Please. Call me Emma."

Baxter tilted his white head. "I once knew an Emma," he recalled. "Lovely woman." His eyes twinkled. "I'll let you have some rest with the little one there. I'm sure you need it more than you'll admit. I'll be in the kitchen if you want anything."

"Thank you." He smiled once again and turned

away, walking sedately across the white ocean of carpet toward the kitchen. "Baxter?"

He turned. "Yes, Miss Emma?"

"You know why I'm here, don't you?" It seemed important suddenly that there be *some* honesty, at least.

"Yes. I know."

She rocked Chandler, taking comfort from his warm weight. "You don't approve."

Baxter's aging eyes studied her for a long moment. "Of you, Miss Emma, I approve wholeheartedly. Kyle, now…well, that's another story. He works too hard, that boy. Always putting off the things that are really important. Reminds me of myself actually. I'd like to see him avoid my mistakes." He smiled and Emma marveled at the way it softened his austere demeanor. "And he wouldn't appreciate my discussing it with you. So I believe I'll enjoy telling him all about it." He tilted his head again in that formal way he had and excused himself on Emma's unexpected choked laugh.

Then Chandler started crying again, and Emma hurried up the stairs with him as quickly as her sore body allowed.

She really did look forward to wallowing in that decadently luxurious square tub. "There are some perks to this crazy arrangement," she told the baby as she settled on the bed to nurse him. "That tub is one of them." Then she closed her eyes, leaning her head against the headboard.

And carefully removed Kyle's presence from the daydream she had of wallowing in that lovely big tub.

Chapter Five

Emma slept for a little while with Chandler, then insisted on unpacking her suitcases herself when Baxter clearly expected to do it for her. She ended up settling Chandler in the old man's arms as a consolation, since he seemed genuinely disappointed that she didn't need his help with her clothing.

He was thoroughly happy with the consolation, however, and once the two males left her room, Emma began to suspect that Baxter had gotten exactly what he'd intended to get all along.

She freshened up in the luxurious bathroom, sat on the bed that Baxter had not been dissuaded from making with fresh linens, and started dialing the white-and-gold princess-style telephone that sat on the end table.

Penny assured her that she would keep an eye on

Emma's belongings at the apartment. And Emma hung up, feeling hideously guilty for letting her friend gush over how wonderfully romantic the whole thing was with Kyle sweeping her off her feet and all. It was obvious that Penny didn't believe Emma's assertion that she'd be back in her apartment after the month was up.

The call to Millie at the diner was no easier. All Emma could do was tell Millie that she *would* take the six weeks that Millie had said she should have, after all. And in the meantime she was spending some time with a friend.

She called her mother and left a message on the answering machine she'd given Hattie two years ago for Christmas. That was much easier, because all she had to do was leave the phone number at Kyle's home with no explanation at all.

Then she called Megan, who assured Emma that she wouldn't broadcast the real reason Emma was at Kyle's. "You're doing the right thing, Emma," her friend said.

Emma wished she could believe that. As far as she was concerned, however, the "right thing" was not accomplished by telling such a whopper of a lie. She was doing the expedient thing. The financially advantageous thing.

She'd sold a chunk of her honesty for the sake of a hospital bill.

"Miss Emma?"

She set aside the phone and looked up to see Baxter in the doorway.

"Kyle just phoned from his car. He'll be here in a few minutes to take you shopping. I've taken the liberty of making sure the little lad's diaper bag is ready for you.''

Emma pushed off the bed and slipped her feet into her sandals, then followed Baxter down the stairs. She nearly looked back to see if they'd left any footprints on that pristine white carpet. ''Where is Chandler?''

''In the kitchen. I believe he likes to be right in the center of things.'' Baxter pointed and sure enough, in the center of the enormous island, Chandler was lying in his springy canvas seat, his eyes wide and alert as he sucked on his fist.

Emma had barely scooped him out of the seat when Kyle arrived. Within minutes they were flying down the road again, this time in the Land Rover Kyle had spoken of.

''We'll drive into Durango,'' he said. ''Okay?''

''Aren't you afraid of running into Mr. Cummings or someone he knows?''

''Durango's not *that* small.'' He shot her a quick look, then returned his attention to the road. ''But you've got a point. We should clear up a few things, just in case.''

''Shall we synchronize our watches, too?''

''Geneva time,'' he said, deadpan.

Despite herself, Emma laughed.

''You've got a nice laugh. You ought to use it more often.''

Outside her window the landscape flashed by. ''My mama told me I'd never find a husband if I couldn't laugh more ladylike.'' Her lips quirked with irony. ''Guess that doesn't count for pretend husbands.''

"Your mother lives in Tennessee, you said."

"Dooley. Population 110."

"Small."

"Well, maybe I exaggerated a little. Dooley's about half the size of Buttonwood. But whereas Buttonwood is a lovely town, Dooley is just…Dooley. A handful of run-down stores, at least a dozen churches and a wealth of people who find nothing more interesting than telling a person that life outside of Dooley simply didn't exist."

"And you thought otherwise. How did your music fit into that?"

She felt his gaze on her hands as if he'd touched her physically, and she realized she'd been absently tapping out the notes of the melody softly crooning from the sound system. And again, his unexpected intuitiveness unsettled her. She moistened her lips and folded her hands. "The only work for a pianist in Dooley is in the bars on Saturday night and the churches on Sunday morning."

"Sinners or saints?"

"Well, the only time one of *those* jobs opened up was when someone died of old age."

"So you ended up in Colorado on the great hunt for musical fulfillment."

She wanted to smile. It would be so easy to like this man. And so very very foolish. Wealthy men whose solution to the challenges of life was to throw money at them. "More or less."

"How many siblings do you have?"

"Five sisters. Two older, three younger."

"Any of them married?"

"All married. What about you? I know you have one sister. The one who had a baby."

"That's Sabrina. She's about your age. Then there's Trevor and Bolt and—"

"Bolt? As in lightning bolt?"

"As in bolting for the door whenever he had to take a bath. If there was a little kid running down the block naked as a jaybird, it was my brother Bolt. His real name is Eugene. Draw your own conclusions."

"I hope he's gotten over that habit," Emma said dryly.

"He says he has." The corners of Kyle's mouth twitched. "But I have my suspicions. The youngest are Felicia and Gillian."

"Are you the oldest?"

"Yes."

"I thought so."

"Why?"

"Just seems to fit." He spoke and people did what he said. Including her.

"I've had a lot of practice at it," he murmured. Then he reached out and with the press of a button, turned up the music. Not enough to disturb Chandler, but definitely enough to signal the end of that particular conversation.

It took her a moment, but then she realized with dismay that she was peculiarly disappointed. She looped her fingers together and looked out the window. Foolish, so foolish. When would she learn her lesson?

She glanced behind her to check on Chandler. He was awake, his eyes wide and inquisitive, and for the moment perfectly content to stare out at the new world around him, even if that new world was the interior of a very well-appointed sport utility vehicle.

"He doing all right back there?"

Emma nodded and faced forward again. Chandler's baby-fresh scent and Kyle's seductive masculine scent combined were heady and unfamiliar, and she rested her head against the seat and silently let out a long breath.

"What about you? Are you feeling all right? Stupid of me not to think you might be uncomfortable riding in the car for any length of time."

The tips of her ears heated. "I'm fine. Lots of extra-strength acetaminophen," she added awkwardly when his gaze rested on her. "Does wonders."

"Mmm."

The silence was broken only by the soft strains of Debussy and the muted rush of wind as they sped along the highway. She drew in the scent of Kyle with every breath she took. "Baxter seems nice," she said somewhat desperately.

"Nice? I guess that might apply on one of his better days," Kyle said dryly. "When he's not being a thorn in my side."

"How long has he been with you?"

"A long time."

Emma thought it was all he planned to divulge. But after a moment he continued. "Bax was a mechanic at the airfield where I learned how to fly when I was fifteen."

Goodness. "I don't know what surprises me more," she admitted after a moment. "The fact that

Baxter was a mechanic or the fact that you were learning to fly at such a young age. I just can't picture your Baxter with grease under his nails.''

''Trust me. Not only did he get grease under his nails, he was one of the best in the business.''

''So how did he end up as your housekeeper?''

''That's a tale you need to ask him about.'' Kyle smiled. ''Bribe him with the offer of holding Chandler. He'll cave in for that, I suspect.''

''And you? Did you really learn to fly at just fifteen?''

''Yeah. Chandler, my dad, had me in a cockpit long before he let me behind the wheel of a car.''

She could see him in her mind. Young, tall for his age, a little gangly perhaps. But still confident. Probably with a healthy dose of cockiness thrown in. Yet he'd spoken so easily of his father, when earlier he'd seemed to fully understand her unwillingness to discuss hers. She must have misunderstood. For why would he name his business after a man he disliked? ''Chandler. Do you actually call him that?''

''Yeah. Lydia is my mom.'' His jaw hardened, then just as abruptly relaxed. ''I went to live with them when I was fifteen. They adopted me when I was seventeen.''

She swallowed her curiosity, even though she desperately wanted to ask him about his first fifteen years. But he'd imparted the information in a flat tone that didn't invite questions.

She angled herself slightly in the seat so that she faced him. ''I suppose you were flying one of those itty-bitty puddle-jumper kind of planes.'' Flying was obviously a safe subject.

"A Cessna. We went up the first time and..."

"And...?"

He shrugged. "I liked it better in the air than on the ground," he said smoothly. "And here we are today."

The words definitely weren't the ones he'd been about to say, Emma was certain of it. "What is it like? Flying? I can't imagine being a teenager and having that control in your hands. Overcoming gravity."

"It's a love affair," he murmured.

"Excuse me?"

"Flying. It's addictive, obsessive, compulsive."

"Sounds rather negative, if you ask me."

"It's also liberating. Exhilarating and profoundly humbling."

He could have been describing the way Emma felt when she sat at a piano and let the music flow from her soul to the keys and back again. Rather than comforting her, though, the striking similarity unsettled her.

She faced forward. "I've only flown once," she said clearly. "It was an enormous airline-jet thing, every seat taken, and the child behind me continually kicked my seat."

"Not an experience you care to repeat."

"No."

"I'll have to take you up myself. You'd feel differently about it."

She imagined sitting in a tiny plane with him and shook her head. "I don't think so."

"You're not afraid, are you?"

Of flying? "No." Of strapping herself into the

close confines of a small airplane, with him beside her, starkly masculine, smelling like every female fantasy. "Not interested."

He just smiled faintly.

Emma decided then and there that she really didn't like the way he seemed to read her mind. Was she so transparent? So obvious?

Just like Jeremy's parents had said?

She looked over at Chandler. *Keep your mind on what's important, Emma Valentine.*

Kyle saw a tangle of emotions flit over Emma's face. He knew how she felt. This wasn't exactly how he spent a lot of time, either, shopping for furniture for a baby's room. *His* baby, as far as appearances went. He took the next exit and parked in the lot outside an upscale furniture store.

"Here?" Emma looked from the long lines of the building to Kyle and back again. "You want to pick out a crib from someplace like this? It'll cost a fortune."

Kyle wasn't sure if he was amused or annoyed. "Are you going to argue your way through every single thing we pick out today?"

Her lips pressed together. Firmly, he supposed. Unfortunately, when she did so, it drew his attention yet again to their soft rosy fullness. And since his curiosity had no business wondering if her lips really were as soft as they looked, he removed himself from temptation.

He got out of the vehicle and went around to the back where he pulled out a spanking-new state-of-the-art stroller. Baxter had arranged it, and now Kyle stared at the contraption and wondered how the hell it worked.

According to Bax, one had only to flip a latch and the whole thing would open up practically on its own. So where was the damn latch?

Emma joined him, touched something near the wheel, and damned if the gray-and-blue monster didn't unfold as easy as you please.

"Now you know how I felt the other day with the car seat." Emma's tone was sweet as sun-warmed honey. She returned to the passenger side and lifted Chandler out of his seat. Then she tucked him in the stroller with a soft blanket, stowed the diaper bag in the area beneath the carrier portion and wrapped her hands around the padded handle. She looked up at Kyle, waiting.

An intermittent breeze lifted a strand of her hair, and the sunshine turned her rich chocolate-brown eyes a paler coffee color. No less absorbing, no less mysterious.

Focus on the goal. Kyle didn't need to actually form the words. They'd been a part of his life for so long they were a part of him.

Focus on the goal.

It had gotten him where he was. It would get him where he wanted to go. Ultimately into Cummings Courier Service, where he could dismantle, disentangle and destroy. And put the past to rest once and for all.

Right now, however, the goal was the furniture dealer and the plan to fill an empty nursery. So he pocketed his wafer-thin cell phone, locked the vehicle and nodded toward the entrance. "Let's do it, then."

Emma's eyes widened. Color stained her cheeks. He knew, at that moment, that her mind had been following the same path as his.

And it most definitely hadn't been toward the purchase of baby furniture. It had been traveling the darkly seductive path of doing *it*. Which was so far outside the boundaries of their agreement it was nearly criminal.

Emma didn't look at him when they entered the store. A soft-spoken salesperson immediately approached and led them through the store to the infant displays.

Kyle looked quickly, uninterestedly, over the offerings. He'd have been content to let the salesperson write up an order for any one of the room displays. But Emma made her way from one thing to the next, peering at the discreet price tags, running her fingers over spindled cribs, gently setting rocking chairs into motion.

He saw the way she kept looking back at one crib in particular. It wasn't anything like the canopied frilly affair his sister had chosen. In fact, it was nearly austere. The beauty of the crib was in the wood. Rich warm mahogany that reminded him of family heirlooms.

Stuff he really knew nothing about.

He had family, sure. Chandler and Lydia Montgomery had been his parents since the day they'd taken in an angry fifteen-year-old and loved him back to life, even though they'd been busy with the family they already had. Their home had been built for func-

tion and simplicity and certainly hadn't run to heirlooms that would be passed down through the gen-
erations. No, what the Montgomerys had passed on
to their kids had been belief in themselves and one
another.

And the home before that? There had been plenty
of heirlooms there, but one by one they'd been sold.
And the lessons learned in that house were ones that
Kyle still struggled against. Despite Chandler and
Lydia.

He caught the salesperson's eye. "That crib
there."

Her eyes lit up and he could practically see the
woman calculating her commission. "Excellent
choice, sir."

"Kyle…"

He turned his attention to Emma. "You like it,
don't you?"

"Well, yes, it's beautiful. But—"

"The matching bureau and that thing there with
the pad on top of it, too." He looped his fingers
around Emma's wrist, and the protests he could see
forming remained unsaid. "What about the rocking
chair?" He looked at Emma.

"Your wife really should try it," the salesperson
said quickly. "Sit and rock your baby for a few moments."

"I'm not his—"

"Excellent idea. Honey, go ahead and try it out."

Emma's mouth closed. Kyle was obviously on a
roll. She sat in the rocking chair.

The salesperson beamed approvingly and excused
herself to begin the paperwork for the order.

"You want to hold Chandler?" Kyle asked.

"He's sleeping." Emma waited until the sales-woman was out of earshot. "Kyle, this is ridicu-lous," she hissed. "What are you going to do with all this stuff when Chandler and I leave?"

"Send it with you."

Her eyebrows rose. "And just *where* would I put it all? You've seen my apartment."

"Get a bigger place. I'll set you up in Eastridge."

"I don't *want* a bigger place in Eastridge. I like living behind Penny. She's a wonderful landlady and a good friend."

He wasn't even paying attention! Emma pushed awkwardly out of the chair and walked right in front of him, propping her hands on her hips. "Now listen to me, Kyle Montgomery. I agreed to—"

"Shh."

Her lips parted. "I beg—"

"The crib's just fine, honey," he said suddenly, his voice several notches louder than usual. "It'll be pretty as a picture in the nursery. But not as pretty as you." His gaze focused on her and he cupped her cheek with his warm palm. "Smile," he murmured in an undertone.

She smiled blindly. Then caught her breath when he suddenly lowered his head and covered her mouth with his.

She reeled.

Honest to goodness reeled. She had to grab his arms to keep from falling backward onto her foolish foolish head. To keep from running.

He pulled back, his eyes searching. His lips hov-ered over hers; she could taste his lips, feel his breath. And she wanted it. Wanted him. Wanted all of him.

"Kyle, darling. I *thought* that was you."

Emma scrambled for a coherent thought when Kyle closed his arm around her shoulder and held her close to his side. She couldn't help but lean into him. And she was grateful for his support, because if it had been up to her unsteady legs, she'd have embarrassed herself.

While she was a noodle, Kyle, however, was as tense as a post. She wondered about it even as she wondered who the brittle woman was who'd called out to Kyle as she wended her way around bedroom suites and armoires toward them.

"Winter," he said smoothly. "This is a surprise. Payton said you were in Vail for the summer."

Winter Cummings, Emma realized. The woman whose advances had apparently started this whole charade. She focused a little more steadily on the chic woman.

Ignoring Emma completely, Winter walked right up to Kyle and tried to kiss him on the lips. But he turned his head slightly and Emma watched his expression turn dark for a moment before it cleared. He was once again smoothly urbane as he wiped the smear of red lipstick from his cheek.

"You haven't met my wife, Winter." Kyle's arm tightened around her shoulders. "Honey, this is Payton Cummings's daughter. Winter, this is my wife—" his tone dropped a notch, sounding slightly rough, definitely sexy and completely adoring "—Emma."

Shivers danced down her spine in the most

alarming way, but Emma smiled. "How nice to meet you. Kyle has spoken of you."

Winter's smile thinned. "And he's rarely spoken of you. I'm surprised we haven't met before now."

Definitely tense, Emma decided. Kyle was very definitely tense. She looked at him, still feeling off balance by that brief kiss. By the fear that she'd truly wanted him to kiss her again. "I've been a bit busy lately," she said in response to Winter's catty comment as she drew the stroller in front of them with one hand.

Winter peered into the stroller, distaste clouding her sharp features. "A baby. Well, well." She arched a perfectly penciled eyebrow. "Kyle, you secretive man, you. What's its name?"

Emma's jaw clenched.

"*His* name is Chandler," Kyle answered.

"Chandler. Now isn't that just…sweet."

"Why, Winter, that's so nice of you." Emma let the comment flow in dulcet tones. "The name has such meaning to us, since it is Kyle's father's name. Of course we couldn't possibly have named him anything else. I'm sure your mama and daddy felt the same when they named you."

Kyle coughed.

"Oh, Kyle, sugar. I hope you're not catching a cold."

"I'm fine." He looked at her, his eyes amused and seemingly indulgent.

What woman wouldn't melt when an impossibly handsome man looked at her so? Emma dragged her attention away from his intense appeal and back to the other woman. "Winter, are you feeling all right? You look rather ill."

"Actually I am a little tired. I guess I'll have to select a new bedroom suite another day." She fluffed her trendy short black hair. "I'll be sure and tell Daddy that I ran into you and…the little woman."

"You do that," Kyle drawled.

Emma nearly jumped out of her skin when his fingers absently threaded through the ends of her hair. Winter noticed the intimate gesture, too. Which meant that it had been worthwhile.

Winter turned and walked away, her hips swaying.

"Thank you," Kyle said after a moment.

"For what?" Now that Winter was gone, Emma had no reason to lean against his side the way she was. Yet she couldn't seem to make herself move. "Acting like your wife?"

"Yes. You were great. I know Winter is a bi—"

"Bit," Emma cut in quickly. "She is a bit… overwhelming."

"A nice way of putting it." He smiled, satisfied. "And I do thank you."

Emma held her breath as his head lowered to hers. She could feel his breath on her temple, on her cheek. On her lips. Oh, goodness, kissing him was…is…

She swallowed hard and stepped back. "I don't think that's a good idea."

"What?"

"Winter isn't watching us any longer. There's no need to, uh, kiss."

He tilted his head. "Yes. You're right."

"Right." She ran her palms down the sides of her skirt. Cleared her throat. "Right."

The salesperson returned then, all smiles at the plum order she'd received without having to do a lick of work to get it.

Emma didn't even bother to protest when Kyle told the woman to add a nightstand and two lovely lamps. She was too busy reliving the moment when Kyle had brushed his lips over hers. Too busy pretending she didn't want to experience it again, despite her protest.

And too busy ignoring the disturbing knowledge that Kyle had wanted to kiss her, too.

Chapter Six

They made several more stops before heading back to Buttonwood. Emma had to excuse herself occasionally to feed Chandler. She wasn't sure why she felt so self-conscious about breastfeeding with Kyle present, but she did.

Under the circumstances it seemed too intimate. Too personal. So she'd found herself a comfortable spot in the ladies' room of a department store where Kyle had decided they'd needlessly expand Chandler's newborn wardrobe, as well as buy bedding and mobiles and stuffed animals for the nursery; in the ladies' room of the surf-and-turf restaurant where they had lunch; and in the cushy back seat of the Land Rover while Kyle met with a man "about an airplane part."

Emma hadn't quite believed that last, but when

they made the return drive to Buttonwood, an enormous greasy-looking thing in a cardboard box was stowed in the back of the vehicle.

Baxter met them at the door with a handful of messages for Kyle, promptly followed with a tsk-tsk for Emma. "Rest for you, miss," he said promptly. "I'll bring you a tray for supper."

Emma glanced at Kyle. He was already focusing on the messages in his hand, walking away. She shifted Chandler. "Thank you, Baxter. That would be very nice."

"Shall I take the little one for a while?"

"I... Yes," she agreed. "I fed him before we drove back, and he's dry for now but—"

"I'll bring him right up to you if he fusses." Baxter delightedly took the baby and waved Emma toward the stairs.

She suddenly felt as if she'd run a marathon. She, whose exercise program before her pregnancy had included regular jogging, weights and cycling, had tuckered herself out completely with one day of shopping.

Baxter had disappeared with Chandler, and Kyle had gone, presumably, to return his calls. He certainly hadn't been tuckered out from the day's activities.

Of course, he hadn't recently had a baby, either.

She looked up the seemingly mile-high flight of stairs and closed her hand over the banister. "One step at a time," she told herself grimly.

From his vantage point in his office, Kyle watched Emma pull herself up the stairs. He didn't often feel like a heel, but he did now. Several times that day he'd felt like a heel. When he'd kissed her, for one. Because he hadn't wanted to stop. When he'd held her pressed against his side because he'd liked, really liked, the feel of one full breast pressed against his ribs.

And when he'd sat across the table from her over lunch and been glad for the cover of the white linen tablecloth as he'd watched her tuck enthusiastically into her meal. He couldn't even remember what they'd eaten. Every time her soft lips had closed over the fork, every time she'd lifted her glass of milk and sipped, every time she'd dabbed the corner of her cloth napkin to her mouth, he'd felt a shaft of heat in his gut.

It was damned inconvenient.

So he'd focused on getting a million tasks done and ended up running the woman ragged.

Even now, even knowing his thoughts were on a road that should definitely be closed, he watched the sway of her hips as she climbed the steps and walked out of sight. He heard the door shut and tortured himself with the vision of her in that big bathtub with nothing but silky water and clinging bubbles covering her creamy skin.

"Sir."

Kyle jerked around, glaring at Bax. The only time his old friend called him "sir" was when he was totally disgusted. Which he didn't need just now. "What?"

Baxter wasn't cowed. "I've prepared a dinner tray for Emma. Perhaps you'd like to take it up to her?"

"If you want to dote on Emma Valentine," Kyle said evenly, "you go right ahead and do it. She deserves all the pampering you can give her. And since you're *preparing trays,* you can bring one in here. I've got work to do.''

Baxter, in black suit and narrow tie and spit-shined wing tips, snorted. ''Work. Demolition, you mean.''

Kyle returned to his desk. He sat down and flipped open a folder of correspondence he'd brought from the office. ''I didn't ask for your opinion, Baxter.''

Baxter followed him. ''Kyle, I understand what you're doing, but it's not going to make you happy.''

Kyle scrawled his signature on the letters and deliberately capped his Mont Blanc pen when he finished. ''I don't recall asking for your understanding, either. Is that Chandler I hear?''

Baxter's mouth snapped shut on whatever unsolicited comments he'd been prepared to voice. He turned on his heel and strode out of the room. Within minutes the soft baby cries had ceased.

Which probably meant that Bax had picked up the baby to take to his mama. Which brought thoughts of Emma front and center all over again.

Swearing ripely at himself, at Baxter, at Payton Cummings, Kyle pocketed his cell phone and strode out of his office. Baxter was on the landing, a tray in one hand and Chandler in the other arm. He pointedly ignored Kyle.

Kyle stomped out of the house, taking his frustration and his gnawing hunger for the woman who now lived under his roof.

He'd assured her that their association would be strictly platonic. She was a brand-new mother, for God's sake. The last thing she needed was a workaholic like him changing the rules on her just because he'd developed a craving to bed her.

But when he climbed behind the wheel of his car, he just sat there, unable to push away the memory of the feel of Emma's lips.

"Damn," he muttered. He could go to the office. He *should* go to the office. Unfortunately, for the first time in Kyle's memory, he didn't *want* to. Bax would undoubtedly get a huge laugh out of it if he knew.

Kyle shoved the key into the ignition and drove down the winding road into Buttonwood. Then he ended up driving aimlessly around as the summer evening darkened.

Hunger eventually led him to Mom & Pop's diner. It was brightly lit and welcoming, and judging by the number of people sitting in the booths, it was popular with locals.

Entering it was rather like stepping into a movie out of the fifties. An old-fashioned jukebox belted out tunes, and several customers were drinking malts through long bendable straws. He felt a pair of feminine eyes studying him as soon as he walked through the door and very deliberately headed for the end stool at the counter.

If he'd felt like being sociable, he'd have stayed home and lusted for his pretend wife.

He shoved his hand through his hair and reached for the laminated menu, even though he wasn't particularly hungry. At least not for food.

Millie Johnson, the woman he'd met at Emma's apartment, was working behind the counter, and she flipped over his coffee cup and filled it. "Nice to see you again. Be with you in a minute."

Kyle nodded, but she had already moved off to deliver an order to one of the couples occupying a booth. He picked up the cup and drank.

Millie returned and leaned her hip against the counter. ''What can I get for you tonight?''

He liked the woman. Even if he hadn't known how she looked after Emma, he'd have liked her. The expression she bestowed on him was as open and honest as…well, as Emma's. ''I hear from Emma that you make a mean blueberry pie.''

''Emma's favorite.'' Millie nodded. ''That it?''

''For now.''

She smiled easily and walked over to the display of pastries and pies. Then she took a few more orders, fussed over a very pregnant young woman who walked in the door, and returned in a minute with Kyle's pie. She'd warmed it and topped it with an enormous scoop of vanilla ice cream, which was slowly melting atop the fragrant pie. ''Let me know how you like it,'' she said. Then she topped up his coffee and set off again.

Kyle watched her. She was constantly in motion. The only time she slowed was when she stopped by the pregnant woman and took her order. ''Rachel,'' he heard her say, ''you need protein, not a hot fudge sundae. I made fresh chicken potpies today. After that you can have dessert.''

The woman, who reminded Kyle a little of Emma because of the brunette hair, laughed, not at all put out by Millie's fussing. ''How about I eat the chicken potpie after the sundae?''

The empty stool beside him was suddenly filled with a female who leaned toward him. Very friendly.

Kyle ignored her and tucked into his pie. It fairly dissolved on his tongue.

"You don't remember me, do you, Kyle?" The woman beside him pouted lightly. She leaned forward again, bringing a whiff of too-strong perfume. "I'm Jessica. Jessica Wilson. I work in Dennis Reid's office. How are you settling into town?"

"Fine." He picked up his coffee cup.

She wasn't deterred. "I know Buttonwood is small, but the streets don't quite roll up at nine. If you're interested in discovering—"

"I'm…involved with someone," he interrupted.

Her eyebrows rose slightly. "Only involved?" She made a production of looking at his hands. "I don't see a wedding ring."

Wedding rings. Damn. Something so obvious, yet he hadn't even thought of it. It wasn't like him. "Nice meeting you, Jessica," he said absently, looking around the woman to catch Millie's attention. He pushed off the stool and went over to the cash register. "Could you pack up a slice of that pie to go?"

Millie nodded. "You bet. Want a little for later?"

"I thought I'd take a piece home to Emma."

Millie went still for a moment. "You're the friend," she murmured. "The one she's staying with.…"

"Excuse me?"

She smiled broadly. "Hang on a second and I'll give you the whole pie."

"That's not nec—" But she was already in action and Kyle closed his mouth.

"You can't stop Millie when she's got an idea in her head."

He realized the pregnant woman, Rachel, was speaking to him. "So I see. You're from the clinic, right?"

She nodded. "Rachel Arquette. And you're Kyle Montgomery. The one responsible for the airlift system we're going to have. Dr. Reid mentioned it to me. It's very generous of you."

Kyle shrugged. "You're a nurse?"

"Guilty as charged. I heard you mention Emma. Valentine?"

"Yes."

Millie returned just then carrying a plain white box.

"Tell her I said hello. The children in peds are looking forward to her coming back again to play piano for them. She and the baby are doing well?"

Aside from being worn-out because of his insensitivity? "They're fine. My housekeeper is doting on them both."

Rachel grinned. "Sounds lovely."

"While you're delivering messages," Millie inserted, "you can tell her to call me. Tomorrow morning. First thing."

"Sure." He pulled out his wallet, but Millie looked at him as if he'd insulted her.

"You're Emma's friend," she said firmly.

"I don't doubt that Emma has lots of friends," he murmured. "And you wouldn't still be in business if you gave away food to all of them."

Millie pushed the pie box into his hands, a smile playing on her lips. "You just deliver the message to phone me, and we'll call it even."

Rachel shook her head, smiling as Millie returned to the kitchen. "Better do as she says."

"I will," Kyle said wryly, and pie in hand, left the diner and walked to his car. His mind was still on wedding rings as he drove out of town and back up the winding road to his house.

He carried the pie into the darkened kitchen. Bax was probably in his room, watching his favorite TV reruns. Kyle cut a chunk of pie, added an uneven scoop of ice cream and carried it upstairs to Emma's room. He tapped on the closed door. Maybe she was already asleep.

"Come in."

His gut tightened as he pushed open the door.

And there she was. Sitting in the middle of the wide bed, her back propped against a stack of pillows and a sheaf of oversize papers spread across her lap. Her hair was damp and curling around her shoulders and her face was scrubbed shiny clean. She looked about eighteen. But the soft yellow nightgown that hung from narrow straps over her shoulders covered a figure that needlessly reminded him that Emma Valentine was most definitely a grown woman. He knew he'd never met a woman whose body shrieked sin and whose lovely face and eyes countered it with such innocence.

"Kyle," she said, those wide innocent eyes expressing her surprise. She set aside the papers. "I thought you were Baxter."

"Disappointed?"

Her cheeks colored and she pushed her hair off her forehead. "Don't be silly."

He started to close the door behind him, then thought better of it. He held up the plate. "A gift."

Her eyebrows rose. "Pie? That looks like—"

"Millie's blueberry pie." He crossed the room and handed it to her. "You were right about it, by the way. Indescribably delicious."

Emma took the plate, carefully avoiding contact with his fingers. "You were at Mom & Pop's?"

"Millie asked me to tell you to call her. Tomorrow first thing."

Her fingers twitched on the plate. "She knows I'm staying here?"

"I didn't tell her in so many words, but she seemed to know. You'd better eat that before the ice cream melts."

Emma obediently took a bite. "Did…did she seem upset?"

"Considering the big smile she gave me? I'd say not."

Emma set the plate on the nightstand. "This isn't going to work," she murmured.

"What?"

"This." She spread her hands. "This charade. All your Mr. Cummings needs to do is walk into the diner where I've worked for a good while now, mention the name Emma, and the truth will get out. Buttonwood isn't exactly overrun with Emmas!"

"Cummings has no reason to go into that diner," Kyle assured her evenly. "He expects me to go to him, not the other way around. Trust me on this, Emma. I know the man's habits. Dropping in at Mom & Pop's isn't one of them. Hell, coming to Buttonwood at all isn't one of them."

"But calling your wife to invite you and her to dinner is."

"What?"

Emma moistened her lips, wishing Kyle would stop hovering over her. "He called this evening. Probably to speak to you, but when Baxter told him you weren't available, he asked to speak to me. To your wife." She'd actually mistaken his voice for Kyle's for a brief moment when she'd picked up the extension.

She watched a muscle work in Kyle's stubble-shadowed jaw. The man was fantasy fodder when he was all spiffed up and clean-shaven. But looking slightly ragged with a definite five-o'clock shadow, he was positively lethal.

"What did he say?"

"You're making my neck hurt. Can't you sit down?" But he didn't sit in the side chair across from the bed. He sat on the edge of the bed, casually nudging her knees over to make room for himself.

"What did Cummings say?"

Emma swallowed and shifted her knees away from his hard thigh. But she only succeeded in brushing the arm that he'd braced to one side. "Winter duly reported the sighting."

"Figures."

"He called to reiterate his invitation to dinner for Sunday night." She wanted to adjust the square neckline of her nightgown, but resolutely kept her hands folded in her lap. "I didn't know quite what to tell him."

"No, I hope."

She looked at him.

"Emma."

"I'm sorry. I did tell him that I thought this week was still a bit soon after the baby and all. But we're on for three weeks from now."

He rubbed one hand over his face and wrapped his other around her calf. "At least there's that. It was going to happen sooner or later. That's why I needed you."

Emma smiled weakly. But all her attention had become focused on the absent way he held her calf. Her bare calf, since her tentlike nightgown had crept up toward her knees.

"Where's Chandler?" he asked abruptly.

"Sleeping." She pointed to the deep wide drawer that was pulled out of the bureau and sitting on the floor.

"Are you serious? We won't wake him?"

"I think he sleeps better with some noise. Take a look." Emma closed her eyes and drew in a long breath when he got up and walked over to see. She also tugged at the bodice of her nightgown. When Kyle looked back at her, her hands were again folded in her lap.

"Cozy," he said softly. "All the stuff we bought today, and your son sleeps in a drawer."

"Like mother, like child," she quipped.

Kyle moved over to her side once more. Thankfully, however, he didn't sit. "Slept in a drawer a time or two yourself?"

"So I've been told. I don't remember."

He smiled faintly. Rubbed his hand over his jaw.

Emma felt her stomach tighten at the brief silence. She drew her legs up, casually tucking the voluminous folds of her nightgown over her knees, covering even her toes. The fabric was opaque, thank goodness.

"How are you feeling?" His eyes drifted over her. From her covered toes to the top of her damp head. Then his gaze met hers. "Are you, uh, doing okay?"

His unexpected concern, oblique as it was, made her throat constrict. "Mmm-hmm. Fine."

"I didn't mean to run you ragged today."

"You didn't. Much," she tacked on when he just kept looking at her.

"For the rest of the week you can take it easy. Indulge Baxter's yen to pamper you. I've got meetings back to back for the next week that'll keep me out of your pretty hair."

She felt her cheeks heat right up through the tips of her ears. "What about dinner with the Cummingses?"

"What about it?"

"What if I can't...can't carry it off?"

A narrow gleam of green studied her from between dark lashes. "You'll be perfect." He reached out and slowly drew a strand of hair away from her cheek. His touch lingered along her jaw, then her chin. "I knew it when I first saw you."

His hand fell away from her face. "You didn't finish your pie."

Emma looked stupidly at the plate on the nightstand. The ice cream had nearly melted, surrounding the vibrant filling with a pool of cream. "Millie makes her ice cream by hand," she murmured. "There's an ice-cream place right by her, but she makes it by hand."

"You're tired, Emma."

Her eyes burned. She looked down at the sheets of music she'd been studying and started gathering them together. "Yes."

He crouched down beside the bed, stilling her restless hands with his own. "Emma."

She froze. He was close enough that she could see the fine webbing of lines fanning out from his mesmerizing eyes.

"I want to kiss you again," he said.

She swallowed. Moistened her lips.

"But I—" his jaw tilted "—won't if you don't want that, too."

"I—"

From his drawer-bed on the floor, Chandler let out a soft cry.

Kyle looked over his shoulder.

The cry built momentum.

Kyle straightened and retrieved Chandler, drawer and all. He lifted it carefully, then set it on the mattress on the opposite side of Emma. "Your son is watching out for you," he murmured. "Good night."

Emma watched him walk out of the room, pulling the door securely closed behind him. She leaned over the drawer and lifted the baby out of the soft nest they'd made from a dozen folded towels. "I wanted to kiss you, too, Kyle," she whispered softly.

Chapter Seven

Kyle sat straight up in bed, blinking in the darkness. His heart was thundering and sweat beaded on his face. He'd dreamed of Emma. Her kiss. Her touch.

It had been too damn vivid for his peace of mind, and even now his nerve endings crawled with the need to taste her again. He looked at the glowing clock and groaned.

Three a.m.

Then he realized what it was that had wakened him from the dream where Emma had been sending him straight to heaven.

Crying. The baby was crying.

It was an alien sound in his home. He let out a rough breath and fell back against pillows that looked as if they'd done battle. He pressed his arm over his eyes, trying to block out the sound of the baby crying.

An alien sound in this home, but not alien to Kyle. And just as he'd been helpless to stop the crying when he'd been a kid, he was helpless now. Little Annie hadn't wanted her seven-year-old brother to cuddle her. She'd wanted their mother, except their mother, Sally, had been out searching for whatever she hadn't been able to find at home.

Chandler continued crying, little bleats of outrage. Kyle unconsciously counted his heartbeats in tune with the pulsing cry. Any minute now Emma would tuck the baby against her breast and the little tyke would…

Continue crying.

Kyle shoved back the rumpled sheet and started for the door. Then backtracked to rummage through his closet for the robe he'd gotten last Christmas from Lydia. He pulled it on, thinking that Emma was the first woman he'd ever bothered to put on a robe for.

Looping the slippery silk belt into a knot, he left his bedroom and looked around the doorway of the nursery, but as he'd suspected, Emma hadn't put the baby in the unfurnished room. He continued on to the connecting room. The door was ajar and he pushed it open.

The only light in the room came from the bathroom. He could easily see Emma pacing, though. Wearing her virginal yellow nightgown that left her shoulders bare but otherwise covered her right to her toes. Chandler was a bundle of blanket and cries on her shoulder.

Even though he was already in the room, Kyle knocked softly on the door to keep from startling her. "Emma."

She turned, her hair swinging with the abrupt movement, then settling like heavy silk against her shoulders. "I'm sorry. I'd hoped we wouldn't wake you."

He banished the dream that still hovered, a sight too real, too disturbing, in his mind, and focused on Chandler. "Is he all right?"

"He's dry and fed and—"

"And you're exhausted." He could hear it in her voice. See it in the angle of her shoulders, the bend of her elegant neck as she lowered her head over Chandler. He still felt guilty over his contribution to that exhaustion. What the hell had he been thinking?

He could have given her a dozen catalogs, and she could have chosen what she wanted from the comfort of a soft chair. But he'd had his plan and that was that.

He walked toward her, grimly aware of the wary look she gave him. "Let me give it a try," he murmured.

"I'm sure I can get him settled."

"I'm sure you can, too, sweetness." He simply reached forward and lifted the baby out of her arms. Chandler wasn't as small as his sister's baby was, but still Kyle could hold him within his two palms. He lifted the infant up to his face. Chandler was so surprised his lips parted, but only a squeak emerged.

Kyle couldn't help grinning at the baby. He was so damn cute with his fists scrunched next to his round cheeks. "You're causing a fuss, big guy," he murmured.

Chandler blinked, wide-eyed.

Beside them Emma sighed and sank onto the side of the bed. "Men," she muttered.

Kyle looked at her. He almost suggested that he take the baby out of her room, but decided against it, figuring she wouldn't appreciate the gesture. Her eyes followed him like a hawk as he picked up the path she'd been making when she'd been the one walking the baby.

"I'm sure you didn't have nights like this in mind when you offered me this, ah…"

"When we decided to help each other out?"

She lifted one silky shoulder. "That's a nice way of phrasin' it," she said, her voice thick with exhaustion.

Chandler squirmed, his legs butting Kyle's chest. Kyle changed his hold, carrying him easily in a football-style grip, the baby's chest and head supported by his forearm and palm. Chandler sighed deeply.

"Though you seem pretty adept at handling babies," Emma added after a moment.

Kyle glanced at her. She'd curled her legs up on the bed and was leaning sideways against the pillows she'd mounded against the headboard. Her face was in shadow, but he could feel her eyes watching him closely. "Little brothers and sisters," he reminded.

"And you're the oldest of them all," she murmured.

He smiled faintly. "Yup." Both the family before Sally's death and the family after. Chandler's eyes were closed, his little bow lips parted slightly.

Emma sank a few inches farther into her nest of

pillows. One narrow strap of her nightgown slipped off her shoulder and hung loosely over her arm. From his vantage point he could see the upper curve of her breast, and he deliberately paced the other way, removing himself from the tempting sight.

"Why Buttonwood, Kyle?"

He heard the rustle of her nightgown, the shifting of pillows, and despite himself, he looked back at her. She'd looped one arm over a pillow and hugged it to her cheek, her chest.

His body stirred. "Why not? I like Buttonwood. It's not overrun with tourists, but it's not a backward little town, either. The clinic is proof of that." He'd been impressed several years ago with the fine services offered by Buttonwood's clinic. So much so that he'd donated a considerable amount of money to it over the years. It was one of the reasons he'd gone to Dennis Reid in his quest for a wife. He knew the man wouldn't advertise Kyle's personal business.

"That's all? You liked it here?"

Chandler was asleep. Kyle kept walking. "Do you want me to give you some great complicated reason?"

"No," she murmured. "Though you do seem more complicated than that."

There wasn't one thing complicated about him at that moment. He was a man, fully aware of a beautiful young woman lying on a bed only three feet away.

Which meant it really was time for him to get out of this room. He moved next to the bed and carefully reached over Emma to settle Chandler in the drawer that was still on the mattress beside her. "He's asleep."

She caught his arm as he straightened. "Thank you."

He couldn't help himself. He ran his thumb along her satiny cheek, leaned over and pressed his lips to her forehead. "You sleep too, sweetness."

She already was.

"Mama, will you let me get a word in edgewise?" Emma propped her elbows on the kitchen counter and held the phone away from her ear. Her mother's agitated chatter went on and on. Baxter, working at the stove across the kitchen from where she sat, lifted an eyebrow.

Emma put the phone to her ear and tried again. "Mama? If you'd listen to your answering machine like I've asked you to do, you'd know I've been staying with a friend. Calling the sheriff to say I was missing was really unnecessary."

Baxter gave her another brows-lifted look.

Emma sighed and shook her head. "My friend Kyle is—" *handsome, intriguing, sexy* "—a perfect host, and *no,* Mama, we're not living in sin." Her jaw tightened and she wished she'd made the call in her bedroom rather than the kitchen, where she'd found herself spending a lot of her time in the past two weeks since she'd come to stay with Kyle. "How is your job at the grocery?" She changed the subject.

Baxter had turned around, facing the stove again as he put the finishing touches on their lunch. Kyle was at work as usual. His statement that she'd see more of Baxter than of him had proved to be true. There were moments she wondered what on earth she was even doing, living in his arctic-white home. As far as she could tell, her ''wifely'' presence had been totally unnecessary.

She listened with half an ear to her mother's comments about work, which Hattie peppered liberally with lectures on life, love and the importance of wearing clean underwear.

Emma didn't know whether to laugh or cry. She pressed her fingers to her throbbing temples. ''Mama, I've got to go now. Mr. Baxter needs to use the telephone.'' She shrugged when Baxter looked at her again. ''I love you. I'll call you again next week.''

She hung up the phone with a clatter. ''I cannot believe she did it. She says she called the sheriff back home in Tennessee. Everybody in Buttonwood knows by now that I'm *involved* with Kyle Montgomery to the point of living with him, but does she call the diner to ask for me there? No, she just keeps calling my home number, and when I don't answer after a few days, she jumps to the most ridiculous conclusion. The sheriff! Can you believe it?''

''What's this about the sheriff?''

Emma whirled around on her stool to see Kyle walking into the kitchen. He set his briefcase on the empty stool beside her and tugged at his tie enough to loosen the button at his throat. ''You're home.''

His eyes crinkled. ''You noticed.''

She forced her lips into a smile, watching him roll up the cuffs of his wheat-colored shirt. He reached past her for the bowl of fruit on the counter and picked up a cluster of green grapes. Emma dragged her attention from his sinewy forearms and focused blindly on the music score she'd been studying before she'd made her weekly call to her mother. But his scent still beckoned, twining appealingly around her senses.

He popped a grape into his mouth and leaned back against the counter. "What's this about the sheriff?"

"Nothing." Emma closed the score and slid from the high stool. Since that first night when, wearing nothing but a dark silky robe, he'd walked her son to sleep, she'd been careful to keep a good amount of physical distance between them. It hadn't been difficult, really. The man was hardly ever around. And when he was, he'd certainly made no gestures toward picking up where they'd left off. He hadn't entered her room late at night again to help her with Chandler when he was fussy. Hadn't mentioned their kiss nor indicated any wish to repeat it.

She still wasn't sure if she was grateful, relieved or insulted.

She crossed to the oversize refrigerator and opened it, then pulled out a bottle of water simply to fill her hands.

"Miss Emma called her mother," Baxter said blandly.

Emma shot him a dark look, which he blithely ignored.

"Which has what to do with the sheriff?"

"Nothing," Emma said cheerfully. "I'm going to check on Chandler." Carrying the water, she strode out of the kitchen and headed for the staircase.

Thoughtfully munching the juicy grapes, Kyle watched her leave. "Okay, Bax. What gives?"

"I wouldn't know, sir," Baxter flipped a pot of curly pasta into a colander and rinsed it under the faucet.

Kyle snorted. "Nothing goes on in this house that you're unaware of."

"Such as the fact that you've spent all of two hours a day here since Miss Emma and the baby came to stay?"

"I've been busy."

Baxter didn't reply; his disapproval was more than plain in his silence.

"You know, Bax," Kyle said conversationally, "I don't *really* have to put up with your attitude. You are an employee."

At that, Baxter laughed, the sound full and unrestrained.

Kyle turned and went after Emma.

He heard her before he saw her. She was singing, her voice low and smooth and rich. He stood in the hallway outside Chandler's nursery and listened.

"Amazing Grace," he realized in the moment before the memory of his mother, his natural mother, singing that very tune sneaked up on him.

She'd often sung to his little brothers and sisters before the accident. Before two-year-old Janice drowned in the big kidney-shaped swimming pool in their backyard. Before his real father had decided marriage and family wasn't for him. After that, Sally hadn't sung anything much at all. Mostly because she'd been too drunk or stoned to remember the words of even the simplest songs.

It had been up to Kyle then to sing to the little kids. Up to Kyle to find some food for them to eat.

And his means had been...creative, since Sally had invariably spent any available cash on her habit.

He brushed away the memories as hurriedly as he'd brushed away the memory of little Annie crying that night he'd helped Emma with Chandler.

He never thought about those days. Not anymore. It only distracted him from the one consuming goal in his life. Taking the sum of Payton Cummings's life's work—his courier service—and erasing its existence from the planet.

Emma was standing in the middle of the room, her long pink skirt swaying as she rocked Chandler and sang. He frowned, wondering when she'd transformed the high-ceilinged room into a cozy colorful haven.

The crib and other furniture they'd chosen that day had been delivered and filled up some of the space in the large room. But it was the yellow-and-blue hanging on the wall above the crib that added some real personality. That, plus the soft matching rugs covering the wood floor.

He looked along the hallway. Pristine white. Glass. Marble. And back into the nursery. Lots of soft colors, warm wood. And Emma and Chandler there in the center of it.

She turned, her brown eyes growing wide when she saw him. Her soft singing was cut off. "I didn't know you were standing there."

He felt strangely reluctant to enter the room. So, of course, that meant he had to. If only to prove he could.

He wandered around, setting the rocking chair into

motion when he passed it, picking up a stuffed bear dressed like a jockey in blue-and-yellow silks.

"Kyle? Are you okay?"

He set down the bear. "Fine. How's your mother? And what's this about the sheriff?"

"Mama's fine. Overreacting as usual."

She briefly explained, but Kyle figured there was a lot of detail she left out. He also figured pursuing it would only upset her.

"What are you doing home this afternoon, anyway?"

"Doesn't Chandler have a checkup this afternoon at the Buttonwood Baby Clinic?"

"Well, yes. But how—"

"I saw your note on the calendar by the phone in the kitchen. I thought I'd drive you. Unless you don't want me to."

"No, no, of course not. I'm just…surprised."

"Why?"

Her soft lips curved and he saw both curiosity and wariness in her expressive eyes. "You're not exactly the kind of guy who does the pediatrician thing, sugar."

"Meaning?"

She eyed him. Firmed her lips and sat in the rocking chair, settling Chandler across her thighs. "Your ease with Chandler is admirable. But playing the dad isn't necessary, you know. Our deal was for me to play your wife for Mr. Cummings's sake, that's all."

"You don't want me to take you and Chandler?"

"I didn't say that."

"Then what exactly did you say, Emma?"

She moistened her lips, pushed her narrow elegant

foot against the floor to make the chair rock slightly. "Just that you don't need to feel obligated to—"

"Obligated?" He smiled faintly. "Emma, honey, you do have one helluva way of making a man feel like a crumb."

"Don't be silly. I was merely—"

"Putting me in my place."

Her mouth opened. Closed. She rocked for a moment. "People in Buttonwood are talking," she finally said. "About me living with you."

"I'm sorry."

She waved one hand. "I expected something like this when I agreed to this insane plan of yours. But, Kyle, it'll only be worse if you take us to our appointment with Dr. Parker at the clinic. Whatever gossip doesn't get traded around the corridors there will be bandied about over pie and coffee at Mom & Pop's for the next two weeks. I don't see any need to add fuel to the fire."

There was nothing wrong with her reasoning. Yet her reasoning had nothing to do with his unrelenting decision to accompany her that afternoon. "Well, as it happens, there's something else we need to take care of at some point, so this afternoon is as good as any since my schedule is already free."

"What do we need to take care of?"

"Wedding rings."

Chapter Eight

Wedding rings.

The pronouncement seemed to echo around the room.

Emma folded her hands together. Protectively, he suspected. Her lashes fell, hiding her eyes from his. "I...see."

"You don't have to wear it until Sunday when we see Payton and his wife."

She was nodding, though. "Couldn't you just, ah, pick something out?"

"I can. But I don't know your ring size."

She moistened her lips, still not looking at him. "Size five," she murmured. Then she stood up, carefully settling the now sleeping Chandler back in his crib.

She headed for the door, but Kyle closed his hand

over her arm as she passed him. "Emma? What's wrong?"

She shook her head, her lustrous brown hair shading her face. "Why, not one single little thing."

He knew her well enough now to know that when she fell into that drawling Southern mode, he'd better tread carefully. He settled his hands on her shoulders, inexorably turning her to face him.

She gave a little shake of her head and looked up at him, her expression closed. "Baxter is probably waiting lunch for us."

"Baxter will forgive us." He touched her satiny chin with his fingertip, lifting her face to his gaze. "What is it?"

She could withstand Kyle in his smoothly urbane CEO mode. She could withstand him in his steamroller get-the-job-done mode. But she couldn't withstand him when his emerald eyes looked at her with such befuddled masculine concern. And she couldn't withstand the fact that he stood so close to her she felt wrapped in his scent, his warmth.

Her eyes burned. "It's nothing. Really, Kyle. Just forget it."

"Too late, honey."

"You don't need to call me that."

His eyebrows drew together. "What? Honey? That's what you're like though, Emma. Rich and smooth with a taste that sweetly lingers."

His gaze on her lips might as well have been a caress for the effect it had on her. An effect that was neither safe nor wise. "The last time I thought about wearing a wedding ring," she said, pushing the words out, "was when I was involved with Chandler's...father.'' As she'd intended, an unmistakable curtain came down over Kyle's intense gaze. Even the hands on her shoulders seemed suddenly less intimate.

"I see," he said smoothly.

Emma bit the inside of her cheek. She'd only told the truth, but it hadn't been the entire truth. And that bothered her greatly. Once a person sold a piece of her honesty, it seemed as if it became easier and easier to prevaricate.

"All right, I'll take care of it," he said, patting her shoulder and dropping his hands.

Emma felt chilled. "Thank you."

He angled his head, gestured to the doorway calmly, as if the moment had never been. "Lunch."

She wasn't the least bit hungry, but she preceded him downstairs. Once again Baxter had set the meal on the lovely table in the garden. She'd eaten lunch out there almost every day. Except this was the first time Kyle had joined her since that first day.

The sun was warm on her shoulders and the sweet scent of flowers surrounded them. Kyle was his typically smooth self.

Just the way she expected, and she felt a good portion of her stress drain away. She was only a woman and he was only her...employer, for lack of a better word.

As he had that first morning, Kyle took the seat with his back to the drop-off. Once Baxter had served their cold pasta salad and fresh rolls and returned to the house, she finally gave in to her curiosity. "Don't you like the view?"

"I bought this place for the view. And the size of

the garage. It held the *Lightning* without requiring any modifications.''

The *Lightning,* she knew, referred to the treasured Lockheed P38 aircraft he was restoring. She hadn't actually seen the thing herself, but Baxter had told her a little about it. About how Kyle had transported the old war plane here, and that the weight of the truck and the plane had put the kibosh on the winding drive, which he was still awaiting a crew to come in and replace. Which, incidentally, meant there still wasn't room for her big orange car.

''But you don't look at the view,'' Emma pointed out, pushing her salad around with her fork.

He looked over his shoulder, then back at her. ''There. Satisfied?'' When he wasn't focusing completely on her, he was focusing completely on consuming the meal before him.

''Baxter is right,'' Emma decided aloud, watching the noonday sunshine glint off his hair. ''You really do work too hard. Do you ever truly relax?''

A faint smile lifted the corners of his mouth. ''Of course.''

''When?''

''I'm not exactly poring over flight routes and FAA regs right now, Emma.''

''And you did loosen your tie,'' she added dryly.

''And I came home this afternoon when the conference call I had scheduled was canceled.''

''So if it hadn't been canceled, you wouldn't have decided you needed to accompany Chandler and me to the pediatrician?''

His eyes crinkled with amusement. ''Is that one of

those female questions I can't answer without putting my foot in my mouth?''

Emma laughed, liking him immensely at that moment. ''You don't have to answer if you'll do me one favor. Trade seats with me.''

He lifted his eyebrows. ''What for?''

''You're an adventurer,'' she said lightly. ''Think of it as a new adventure.''

He reached over and pressed his palm to her forehead. ''No fever.''

Emma stood up, gathering her plate with hands that trembled slightly. She hadn't expected that touch. It was one thing when she was expecting it. She could brace herself, prepare herself for it.

''Why on earth would you call me an adventurer?''

She walked around and stood behind him, tapping her bare toes with exaggerated impatience.

''You're a pilot for one thing,'' she said as he finally shoved his plate around to the other side of the table. ''A successful businessman in a rather atypical business. Moving your business to this area from a tried-and-true location. That all seems adventuresome to me. And of course, there's that babe-magnet you race around in.''

She took his seat, smiling. ''There. What do you think?''

Kyle looked across at her. The spectacular view behind her shoulders was nothing compared to the view of her. In the past two weeks, she'd regained an incredible amount of energy. She fairly radiated health and vitality, and he couldn't be within arm's reach of her without finding himself beating back the urge to taste her lips again. To press every inch of her creamy body to his.

She was waiting for a response.

"I think the view is way too distracting for my peace of mind," he said truthfully.

Her brows drew together. "You're the type of executive who faces his desk away from the window, or the doorway, or the hallway, I'll bet. So you can focus exclusively on your work."

"And you look at the world around you and see music in every single dust mote."

"Well, sugar, no wonder our marriage is so successful." She let the words flow lazily.

He was hard. She'd spoken in the tone that fairly oozed hot lazy afternoons and tangled sheets, and that was all it took. Dammit.

He reached for his glass of iced tea and chugged it.

"You all right?" She moved his untouched glass of ice water toward him. "Did you swallow wrong? I don't need to do the Heimlich maneuver on you or something, do I?"

Kyle wanted to laugh. "Or something," he muttered dryly. "I'm fine. Just hot."

She smiled. "It is warm out here in the sunshine." She pushed her nearly untouched plate out of the way and rested her arms on the table, her fingers linked together. Her wavy hair brushed over her lightly tanned shoulders as she turned her head to look back at the view she'd just traded away.

Thanks to Baxter's relentless updates, Kyle knew that Emma spent quite a lot of her time working in the overgrown garden and taking Chandler for daily walks up and down the winding road leading to the house. And the lighter streaks of brown threading through her shiny hair and the golden cast to her skin bore out Baxter's stories.

"I think the heat feels marvelous, though," she was saying. "It's days like this that I dream about during the winter when I can't seem to get warm enough."

Kyle dragged his eyes from the enticing shadows at the scooped neckline of her sleeveless vest. He'd always considered himself more of a leg man, but Emma's curves were seriously hindering his sanity. Thank God he hadn't seen any more of her perfect legs than he had.

"Sir."

His attention was jerked to Baxter, who was eyeing him knowingly. Who needed a conscience when Baxter was right at hand? "Yes?"

"There's a call for you."

"Who is it?"

"Your father."

Emma saw Kyle's quick frown. He tossed his napkin onto the table and strode inside.

"Not hungry, Miss Emma?"

"It's delicious, Baxter," Emma assured him. "I guess I'm just a little nervous about this afternoon. Taking Chandler to the doctor and all."

"Mmm." Baxter began collecting plates.

Emma rose to help him. He'd finally given up on telling her he didn't require her help with the household tasks. "Mmm," she said, imitating his tone impeccably. "What, exactly, is that supposed to mean?'' She followed him into the house and set her load on the kitchen counter.

''I didn't notice any particular nervousness about the appointment earlier today,'' he said smoothly.

She propped her hands on her hips. ''I swear, Baxter, you beat around a bush better than anybody I know. You sure you're not from the South?''

''Buffalo, New York, I'm afraid.''

Emma waited a moment longer, then tossed up her hands. ''Baxter, I'm warning you—you'd better stop being so cryptic around me or I'll decide that Chandler really doesn't need to spend those two hours every morning with you.''

Baxter looked horrified. ''Miss Emma, I—''

She laughed lightly and kissed his aristocratic cheek. ''Relax, Baxter. I'm just teasing you.''

He relaxed. ''Dirty pool,'' he declared.

''You betcha.'' She headed out of the kitchen, looking over her shoulder for a moment at the housekeeper. ''Just like you do with Kyle,'' she said pointedly. Then she had the pleasure of hearing Baxter's laughter follow her as she went upstairs to freshen up before she took Chandler into town for his appointment.

She was standing in front of the wide bathroom mirror pulling her hair back into a ponytail when she realized she wasn't alone.

Her eyes met Kyle's briefly in the mirror, and she lowered her gaze, quickly finishing with her hair. ''How's your father?''

''Fine.''

Emma squared the handle of the brush with the matching comb, braced herself mentally and turned to face him. She'd already put on her shoes, and the small bit of heel brought her eyes a little closer to the level of his shoulders, but he still seemed tall and broad and...

In her way. She focused on the loosened silk tie at his strong throat. She felt like a yo-yo around him. One minute comforted by his presence, the next trying not to tremble because of the shivers he set off down her back with one glance. She moistened her lips. "What is it?"

"Winter has struck again."

Winter. Winter who'd kissed him as if she'd done it many times before. But, she reminded herself, Kyle hadn't exactly encouraged her that day in the furniture store. "Winter Cummings?"

"Apparently she goes to the same fitness center as a friend of one of my sisters."

"Oh, dear."

"When the story reached her, Felicia was smart enough not to let on that her big brother certainly *wasn't* married with a new baby, but she didn't waste any time getting on the horn to the folks." He didn't betray his irritation by so much as a twitch of a muscle, but Emma could tell he was rigid with it. "As a result, Chandler said he and Lydia decided to cut short the cruise I sent them on and come to visit."

"Your parents are coming?" The thought sent horror coursing through her and she pressed a nervous hand to her chest. "Here?"

"I talked him out of it for now."

Emma let out a relieved breath. "Thank goodness. I mean there is a limit to how much playacting I can do."

"You don't think you could fool my folks?"

Her nerves prickled. "Well, of course not. You wouldn't want to, right? And—and there'd be no need to. You'd just tell them how you're buying Mr. Cummings's company and—"

"No."

She blinked. "Excuse me?"

"My parents don't know. And they're not going to know."

"Why not?"

His lips compressed. "It's complicated."

And none of my business, Emma finished silently. She suddenly felt awkward, ridiculous, standing there, hemmed in the luxurious bathroom. She was only the hired wife. So it was ridiculous to feel hurt.

But she was. And no amount of pretending would make it otherwise.

"Well, I'm sure you know best." She stepped forward, lightly pushing her hands against him to move him out of the way.

Except he didn't move. Not out of her way. He raised his hand and captured both her wrists, holding them captive against his wheat-colored linen shirt. Captive against the hard chest beneath, warm and strong and pulsing with the heavy beat of his heart.

Emma focused desperately on their hands. "Kyle—"

"I think we could fool my folks," he murmured.

Her cheeks heated. "As you said, there's no need."

"No, actually. You said that."

"Well…regardless, it's a moot point. The situation—" his thumb rubbed slowly over the sensitive flesh of her inner wrist, sending her pulse skittering "—isn't going to, um, occur." She tugged weakly at her hands, but he still held her fast. Drew her closer. "Kyle—"

"We've got a problem, Emma."

"Of course we do. We're livin' a lie."

"I thought if I ignored it, I could make it go away. Pretend it didn't exist. Stupid. I usually know better."

She swallowed. She couldn't pretend she didn't know where he was going with this. That she had such an effect on him was something she'd have to take out and examine at another time. Right now she was having enough difficulty not letting her body soften against his. Not pressing herself against him and—

She cut off the tempting utterly foolish thought. He was a wealthy man who truly believed that every situation could be solved with money. "You said…" Her throat tightened around the words. "You promised me that things would, ah—" she broke off when he lifted her hand and pressed his lips to her inner wrist.

Her head swam. Good gravy, didn't she ever learn her lesson?

She yanked her hand free, scrambling inelegantly back until she thumped her rear against the marble vanity. "Platonic," she blurted, her entire body raging with heat. "You promised."

A muscle twitched in his jaw. "Yes, I did." He raised one hand, wrapping it around the doorjamb above his head. "I—"

"Just because I've obviously…been with one

man, seeing as the proof is sleepin' in the nursery, that doesn't mean I'm going to hop into bed with you, even if you are catnip to a girl like me. So if that's what you've had in mind, you can forget this whole crazy idea right this instant. I may be foolish, but I'm not easy.''

''You sure in hell aren't,'' he agreed. ''I never once implied you were promiscuous.''

Embarrassed, annoyed, and still shaking because she couldn't recall ever wanting to be with Jeremy St. James quite as badly as she wanted to feel Kyle's body against hers, Emma crossed her arms tightly across her chest. ''If you want some good lovin', I'm sure Winter Cummings would be happy to accommodate you again,'' she drawled, desperate to put some distance between them. Not physical distance, either. Though that wouldn't hurt any.

His eyes narrowed and he dropped his arm from the doorway. ''Again?''

''I could tell that day in the furniture store that you and she have...been together.'' Regardless of what he'd led the other woman to believe about his marital status.

''You think Winter and I have been intimate?''

She forced a casual shrug. ''I say easy, you say promiscuous. I say together, you say intimate. Sugar, even if I was inclined to...'' She unfolded her arms long enough to wave a vague hand. ''Well, I am the black sheep of my Tennessee family. I'd know better than to set my sights on a country-club type like you who probably doesn't even own a pair of blue jeans.''

She thought for a moment she'd gone too far. His

green eyes turned to chips of stone and his lips compressed. Her stomach fluttered, but not with fear.

Then his lips softened and his rigid stance eased.

The flutters gained speed.

He came toward her, his movements lazy and screaming, "Dangerous man approaching." She took a hasty step back, but the marble vanity wasn't budging.

One corner of his mouth curled. "For a black sheep you look a mite nervous, honey."

She unfolded her arms and pressed her hands to either side of her, tilting her head back bravely. Even when he stepped right up to her, invading her personal space and encompassing her with his sensual scent.

"You're a babe in the woods in comparison to a man like me," he murmured. "And your ridiculous notion about Winter and me aside, I do like the way you cut to the chase." Between his dark lashes, his narrowed eyes held a primitive gleam. "I want you. In my arms. In my bed. Under me. Over me."

He ran his thumb along her jaw and all her bravado died a hasty ignominious death. She trembled, knowing that at that particular moment nothing could prevent what he described so simply, so devastatingly. Not even the fact that Chandler wasn't yet a month old.

Then his hand dropped and he stepped away. Emma blinked. The dangerously prowling male had been replaced with the dangerously smooth male.

"But I like you," he said quietly, "so I won't do that to you. Just don't poke that sleeping dragon too hard, Emma. When he awakens, it's not easy to get him back to sleep."

Chapter Nine

Emma endured the drive to Buttonwood in silence. If asked, she wasn't sure she could put a name to what had transpired between Kyle and her in the luxurious bathroom. All she knew was that somehow something had changed.

She'd been so certain she had Kyle pegged. Yet he kept popping out the sides of the tidy box that her mind, her sense of security, had fitted him in.

And the fact that she'd had such preconceived beliefs about a man she'd met less than a month earlier horrified her. Heaven knew how many occasions she'd chafed at the opinions people formed about her without ever actually knowing her.

One more welfare kid of Hattie Valentine's. The teenager who never quite fit in because she doodled with Handel and Rachmaninoff when her classmates were listening to Foreigner or Billy Ray Cyrus, sneaking their daddy's smokes and joyriding on Friday nights.

The cheap little Southerner who'd tried to trap golden boy Jeremy St. James into marriage by getting in the family way.

None of which was really *who* she was any more than she could be certain silk ties, gold watches and alligator boots were who Kyle was.

Life was just too confusing sometimes.

When they drove by Mom & Pop's diner, Emma stifled a sigh. She missed the familiar. Missed her days, long as they'd often been, that she'd spent serving up coffee and pie and chicken fried steak to her regulars. Many who came from the complex across the street. Goodness knew Millie's food was ten times better than anything served up over there in the cafeteria.

Kyle parked and Emma surreptitiously watched him round the vehicle to open her door.

"Do you want to get Chandler or shall I?" His voice was perfectly ordinary. As if nothing had happened between them at all.

As if she hadn't stood beside him in her bathroom and felt the waves of desire emanating from him.

"Maybe you could get the stroller," she suggested faintly.

He nodded and went to the rear of the Land Rover to pull out the stroller. Emma deftly unfastened Chandler, then turned to place him in the stroller when Kyle brought it up next to her. He slipped the strap of the diaper bag from her shoulder and looped it a few times through his fist, then walked with her toward the clinic.

They could have been any ordinary couple, taking their new baby in for a checkup. But once again appearances were deceiving.

Kyle stayed at her side right through the brief examination that set Chandler into an outraged crying fit from start to finish. Emma felt like crying herself by the time they were finished.

She cradled Chandler to her shoulder, trying to comfort him as Dr. Parker made some final notes on Chandler's chart. Kyle stood near the closed door, one shoulder leaning against the wall, decorated in cheerful blue and red. One hand was pushed in the pocket of his perfectly pleated trousers, and she would have thought he was as calm as Donald Parker was in the face of Chandler's outrage. But she could see the muscle jump in Kyle's jaw.

"Good set of lungs there."

Kyle gritted his teeth when Dr. Parker grinned and patted Chandler's back, his hand touching Emma's slender one. He suddenly straightened from the wall and settled *his* hand on Emma's shoulder. He'd had enough of Parker's none-too-subtle friendly overtures toward Emma. "Are we finished here?"

Dr. Parker's brown eyes studied Kyle for a moment, seeming to take his measure. Then he clicked his pen, pocketed it in the front pocket of his white lab coat and folded up the baby's medical file. "All set," he said easily. "Emma, give me a call if you need me, but that little boy of yours is in great shape. And in great hands."

Kyle knew how Emma worried about every little

hiccup of Chandler's, so he told himself it was rea-
sonable that her shoulders would relax at the doctor's
assurance. But he still didn't like the way the other
man was looking at Emma. He pulled open the door
to the examining room, grabbed the diaper bag and
ushered Emma and Chandler out into the corridor.

He headed straight for the appointment desk so he
could make arrangements for the bill and they could
get out of there.

"Kyle." Emma pulled back. "Where's the fire?"

He slowed his steps, realized his fingers were too
damn comfortable cupping the silky curve of her
shoulder and dropped his hand. "There's no reason
to hang around, is there?"

Her eyes didn't meet his. "There's no reason to
race out of here like the devil is at our heels, either."

He handed the nurse behind the desk his business
card. "Send the bill there," he told her, then turned
to face Emma. "You like that guy coming on to
you?" he asked softly.

She looked at him then. Her lips parted. "Who?"

"Donald Parker."

Emma's eyebrows skyrocketed. "You must be
joking. He wasn't—"

"He was."

Aware of the attention they were garnering, he put
his hand on Emma's arm and escorted her through
the waiting room where the stroller was. He dumped
the enormous diaper bag into the stroller and pushed
it one-handed toward the exit.

Emma waited until they were in the main lobby.
"Just because Dr. Parker is friendly doesn't mean he
has designs on me," she said stiffly. "Good heavens,

the man has nurses tripping over themselves to have a chance at him.''

"He wasn't thinking of nurses when he was looking at you," Kyle assured her. "Trust me, honey, I know where his mind was."

"You're being ridiculous. He is a professional! He wouldn't—"

"He's a man."

Her soft lips compressed. Color ran high in her cheeks. "A person might think you're feelin' jealous, with all the fuss you're causing."

"You're supposed to be my blushing wife," he reminded softly. "The last thing I need is word getting out that my *wife* is seeing Dr. Lothario."

Every drop of color drained from her face. She moved the diaper bag and settled the baby in the stroller. And without a word, she strode out of the building, silent pain shrieking from her with every swish of her skirt around her ankles.

Dammit to hell.

He started after her.

"Kyle? Kyle Montgomery?"

He looked at the middle-aged woman who'd entered the building only moments after Emma had exited. "Helen," he greeted, hiding his consternation as he recognized Mrs. Payton Cummings. "What brings you here?" And how the hell had he not known she frequented the clinic?

"A friend of mine works here," she said, smiling pleasantly. "Payton and I are looking forward to having you and your wife join us on Sunday. Is she here? Winter tells me you two have recently had a child."

"I'm joining her shortly," he said not untruthfully.

She tilted her stylish salt-and-pepper head. "I feel so silly that we were unaware you were married."

Kyle's nerves tightened. "Emma prefers not to get involved with the business." He realized that could be taken in a not entirely flattering way. "She's working toward her degree in music," he added.

Helen's blue eyes softened. "I do find it lovely when a man can be proud of his wife's accomplishments even when they aren't mirrors of his own." She clasped her hands together over her purse. "How long have you been married?"

Kyle tucked his clenched hand in his pocket. "Not quite a year."

"Newlyweds." She sighed happily. "You *must* bring your wedding photos on Sunday," she declared. "I simply adore looking at wedding photos." Her lips pursed. "Since Winter shows no signs of wanting to walk down the aisle anytime soon, I have to have somebody's wedding memories to pore over."

She glanced at her watch, completely unaware of the pillar of stone Kyle had turned into. "I've got to run." She gave Kyle's arm a motherly pat. "Until Sunday. And don't forget those photographs."

Kyle watched her walk toward the elevators. Managed to smile faintly and sketch a return wave before the elevator doors shut and carried her safely out of sight.

He raked his fingers through his hair and headed out into the bright sunshine. The delay had been only minutes, but Emma had been moving, fast and furious.

He didn't blame her.

But he did have a good idea of where she'd gone.

He headed down the street to Mom & Pop's.

Emma was breathless by the time she pushed the stroller through the door of the diner. Millie, in her customary position behind the counter, spotted Emma right away. "You brought the baby!" she cried, delighted.

She set down the coffee carafe and hustled around the counter, giving Emma a quick hug before leaning over the stroller. "Oh, please tell me I can hold him."

Dear Millie. So familiar, so wonderful. Emma felt her eyes sting and nodded. "Sure."

Millie's eyes lingered on Emma for a moment, then she turned her attention back to Chandler. He'd stopped crying as soon as she'd tucked him into the stroller and made her mad dash for the diner, and now he was bright-eyed and positively charming as Millie picked him up and carried him around to the regular customers, as proud as any grandmother.

Prouder, Emma corrected silently. Goodness knew her own mother had been less than pleased with Emma's pregnancy. As Millie showed off her little "sweet pea," as she called Chandler, Emma folded up the stroller and set it out of the way of the door, then headed toward one of the empty booths. The lunch rush had passed, and about half the diner was occupied.

She'd just slid into the booth when two women stopped next to the table. Emma looked up, squelching a sigh. "Hello, Flo. Blanch. How are you today?'' Florence Harris and Blanch Hastings had good hearts, she knew. But she didn't think there were any two women in Buttonwood who knew more about other people's business than they did. And the ladies, now in their sixties, seemed to take great pleasure in making sure everyone knew their opinions, too.

They slid into the bench opposite Emma. ''Is it true?''

Hidden under cover of the table, Emma clasped her hands tightly. ''Is what true?''

''That you're living with that man,'' Flo said, her hair practically bobbing with her agitation. ''Blanch told me, but I said right back to her, 'Blanch, that can't possibly be so.' ''

''That's right,'' Blanch agreed. ''She said that.''

''Since we all know you were crazy in love with that law student last summer, I just assured Blanch that you wouldn't go from the frying pan into the fire.''

Emma's mouth parted, ready to respond. Somehow. Some way. But Blanch hadn't finished.

''I hear *he* wants our little airport to be the next Denver Stapleton.'' Blanch leaned over the table toward Emma. ''Is it true he donated all that money to the clinic? That his sheets are silk and he has caviar for breakfast in his fancy house up on the mountain?''

Flo tsked. ''Oh, Blanch, don't be ridiculous.'' She focused her intense gaze on Emma. ''You're too innocent for your own good, Emma dear. If your mother was here, she'd surely counsel you not to become involved like this with another man so soon after…well, after that unfortunate business last summer.''

Emma flushed. She looked over at Millie, hoping for rescue, but Millie was busy introducing Chandler to one customer while she served up chicken soup to another.

"A man won't buy the cow if he can get the cream for free," Blanch said.

Kyle's insults were easier to take than these busybodies' counsel, no matter how well intentioned. But if she said anything to the two women, anything at all, Emma knew her words would make it through the town's gossip mill faster than a three-eyed rat running through a cheese factory.

"Oh, dear me!" Blanch exclaimed. "That's him, isn't it?"

"Handsome one," Flo added.

Emma swallowed, deliberately keeping herself from looking toward the door. She didn't need the ladies' comments to know that Kyle had entered the diner. She could *sense* him. Her nerves tightened and the hair at her nape prickled.

"He's coming over here!" Blanch squeaked.

"Good afternoon, ladies," Kyle said smoothly.

Flo sniffed, her eyes raking Kyle. "Taking advantage of an innocent young woman," she muttered. Then her eyes flashed on Emma. "And you, Emma Valentine. It's no wonder Emil Craddock had to let you go from your teaching position at Benderhoff. What kind of example are you setting for those impressionable children, openly living the way you are with a man? A newcomer to Buttonwood, furthermore.''

Emma wanted very badly to tell the woman that Emil Craddock had canned her *before* she'd taken her sinful ways up the mountain to live in Kyle Montgomery's fancy house.

"Emma doesn't need to work at Benderhoff," Kyle said smoothly, sliding into the booth beside Emma. His hip burned against hers, but he closed his arm around her shoulders before she could slide farther over. "Now that she's my wife, she can concentrate on finishing her degree."

Emma's eyes flew to his. He was smiling at her, his green eyes hard. He dropped a light kiss on her numb lips, then casually looked across the table to see the reaction his statement had caused the two women.

They were staring, their jaws slack.

And Emma realized with dismay that *everyone* in the diner was staring at them. Kyle brushed his fingers over her cheek. "Did you want to have some blueberry pie before we drive home?"

Emma couldn't have swallowed food right then if her life depended on it. Not even Millie's pie. "No," she managed to say. "I'm ready to go." She was glad no one looked at her ringless hand. She wouldn't have thought about it except for Kyle's earlier comments.

He smiled indulgently. "You'll excuse us, ladies, won't you? I don't like Emma to overtire herself."

At any other time Emma might have enjoyed the speechlessness of Flo and Blanch. She let Kyle take her hand and help her from the booth, then tried not to stare too hard when Kyle retrieved Chandler from

Millie. Her boss caught her in a hug before she could unfold the stroller.

Conversations had returned to normal in the busy diner, thank heaven, and so Emma was reasonably certain Millie's "We're going to talk, young lady" wasn't overheard.

Kyle settled Chandler in the stroller, then took Emma's cold hand and ushered her out of the diner. She waited until they were across the street and hidden by the cars in the parking lot before yanking her hand out of Kyle's grasp. She'd been such a fool to agree to his insane plan.

"Nothin' good ever comes from a lie," she muttered, stalking to the passenger door of the Land Rover.

Kyle set the brake on the stroller and caught her shoulders in his hands, turning her inexorably toward him.

She hated the knowledge that, as hurt and angry as she was, she still couldn't help noticing his powerful forearms, revealed by the rolled cuffs of his wheat-colored shirt, or the hollow at the base of his throat, exposed by the two buttons he'd unfastened. "What is it, Kyle?" Her throat felt raw. "You want to lecture me some more to make sure I don't embarrass you by acting like an improper wife? Boy, imagine their surprise if they *really* knew the truth."

"Stop."

"Why?" Her laugh was brittle. "I should've known better, of course. You're cut from the same privileged cloth as Jeremy. And he'd wanted my body, too, just like you. But I wasn't good enough for anything more. I didn't carry the right pedigree and I might damage the family name with my scarlet behavior.''

"I shouldn't have said what I did about Parker," Kyle said, his voice rough. "But I want you to stop talking about yourself that way. That is *not* what this is about at all."

"Oh, really? I just imagined that you accused me of being unfaithful?" Her lips twisted. "So ironic, of course, considering there's nothing between us for me to be unfaithful to."

"That's the problem, sweetness, there *is* something between us and you know it as well as I do. The very thing that makes you so perfect to be my wife is the very thing that is sending us both around the bend."

"I'm an adult," she said tightly. "I think I can control myself from throwing myself at you or Dr. Parker or any other man who looks my way."

"Dammit, Emma, that's not it, either." He propped his hands on his lean hips, bowing his head for a moment. "I'm not sure I can control myself," he finally said. "I told you earlier today how I felt. And I meant what I said, Emma. You're safe from me." He shook his head. "But I didn't like the way Parker looked at you. Pure and simple. 'Cause he looked at you the way *I* look at you. Like a woman he wants."

She swallowed past the knot in her throat. "He may want," she said thickly, "but that doesn't mean he's going to *get*. You *hurt* me," she admitted flatly.

"I didn't mean to, Emma. I'm just… Damn. I'm not good at this sort of thing."

"Pretending to be married?"

"Letting someone into my life."

Her lips parted. She moistened them. "Then we have no problem at all," she countered. "Because you didn't let me into your life. You hired me to play a role."

He slammed his hand against the hood of the Land Rover and Emma gasped. "You know what I wish? I wish I'd married you for real," he growled in a low voice. "Because then I wouldn't have the conscience that was drilled into me by Chandler and Lydia Montgomery to contend with. I'd have you in my bed, even if we couldn't *really* be together quite yet because of the baby. There are dozens of ways to make love, sweetness, and I'd make sure we devoted plenty of time to discovering each and every one of them."

Emma dragged her eyes from the dent he'd left in his vehicle, his words ringing in her ears. "What you want more than anything," she corrected, "is to complete your deal with Mr. Cummings, and if it wasn't for that, you and I wouldn't be having this conversation at all. You wouldn't have looked twice at a woman like me."

He shook his head again. "We've got to do something about this self-image thing of yours, Emma." A car drove slowly past. Then stopped and backed up.

An elegantly coiffed woman rolled down her window, a smile on her face. "Kyle. Is this your lovely wife?"

Kyle clamped his hand around Emma's wrist and drew her toward the idling car. "Yes. Emma, this is

Helen Cummings. We ran into each other while you were at the diner.''

Emma thought she managed a smile. She wasn't sure. But Helen Cummings was smiling wide enough for both of them. "It's such a delight to meet you, Emma," Helen said. "I know we'll have a lovely time this weekend when you and Kyle come up to see us. Payton thinks so highly of Kyle." She laughed lightly. "I made Kyle promise to bring your wedding photos."

"But—" Kyle's arm about her shoulders tightened warningly.

"I won't forget," he assured her smoothly. "You drive carefully."

With a wave Helen took off.

Emma leaned back against the sun-warmed car. "I'm not up to this," she said, feeling frantic at the way her life was snowballing out of control. She looked up at Kyle. "Wedding photos? You couldn't have told her that we eloped or something?"

He made a rough sound. "She caught me off guard," he said. "Had I not been thinking how satisfying it would be to wrap my hands around Donald Parker's throat, I might have been thinking a little faster on my feet."

Emma sighed. She was exhausted. Physically. Emotionally.

And it didn't help that nothing had really been resolved. "I won't sleep with you, Kyle." She stared down at her twisting hands. She didn't even like acknowledging the fact that she wanted to. She looked over at Chandler, content in his stroller. "I don't regret my son. But I won't be so unwise with my heart ever again. Not even with you.''

She only wished she could be certain she could live up to her words.

Chapter Ten

"Kyle said he'll meet you at the airport, Miss Emma."

Emma nodded and finished fastening Chandler's fresh diaper. "Thank you, Baxter."

"Are you sure you don't want to leave the lad with me while you go to Denver?"

Emma smiled gently. "I'm not ready to leave him overnight. But I promise you'll have first dibs when I am."

Baxter smiled. "Good enough, Miss Emma."

He followed her down the white stairs. It was Friday morning, and Kyle was flying them to Denver to take care of the little problem of a wedding photo album.

Emma had barely been able to sleep the night before, wondering just exactly how Kyle thought he

was going to "take care" of anything. All he'd told
her was to be ready for an overnight stay.

Since their encounter with Helen Cummings outside the clinic, they'd both gone out of their way to
avoid being alone with each other.

Kyle had an easy solution for that, of course. He
left for the office well before dawn and didn't return
until well after dark, just as he'd done since they'd
entered into their unorthodox arrangement.

Emma didn't think so highly of her own appeal
that she considered Kyle's long hours to be an avoid-
ance tactic. He was simply an extremely busy man—
the head of a thriving company and one of the state's
major employers, so she'd discovered when she'd
made it a point to learn more about her "husband."
She'd also found out that he'd been accurate when
he said he kept his private life private. Nowhere had
she found anything that concretely said he did or
didn't have a family. Immediate, adoptive, birth or
otherwise.

Since Kyle had been scarce, Emma had spent a
good portion of her time wondering what on earth
she had in her wardrobe that wouldn't appear inappropriate in wedding photos. She'd finally settled on
an off-white blazer that she fancied up with a sheer
ivory scarf tucked in along the collarless neckline.
The scarf also conveniently disguised the fact that
the jacket, which buttoned past her hips, displayed a
bit too much cleavage for comfort. With it, she wore
an ankle-length skirt with minuscule pleats.

Though she felt as if she looked like she was ready
to attend Easter worship, Baxter had assured her that
she looked "quite lovely." She could've kissed him

for his sweetness, because he'd known she was nervous as a cat.

When they arrived at the airport, entering a key-accessed lot behind some buildings, Emma felt like a wreck. Kyle's car was parked under a shade structure.

Then the man himself walked out of a rear door of the building, writing on a clipboard. He handed the clipboard to the man beside him, then strode toward the Land Rover.

She felt dizzy. She simply couldn't forget Kyle's saying he wanted to make love to her. It was always there with them. Like a physical presence.

Kyle reached the vehicle and opened her door. "Thanks for driving them out here, Bax," he greeted. His attention rapidly switched to Emma and he helped her from the vehicle. "It's been a hectic morning," he murmured. "You look very nice. But a bit pale. Afraid to go up with me?"

She smiled shakily. If he wanted to attribute her pallor to fear of flying, that was okay with her.

Baxter handed over Chandler with a sigh. "You're sure you're not ready for a vacation from the baby yet?"

Emma had to laugh. "Quite sure, Baxter."

Kyle pulled her overnight case and the diaper bag from the vehicle. "We'll be back tomorrow," he told Baxter, then placed a hand at Emma's back and ushered her into the building.

Emma barely gained the impression of busy offices, clacking printers and chatter as Kyle hustled her through the building and out the other side toward a sleek airplane that looked nothing like the two-seater she expected.

A svelte young woman with a perfect smile and showgirl legs greeted them when they reached the top of the rolling staircase. "Good morning, Mr. Montgomery." She smiled, blindingly white, at Emma. "Everything is ready for your flight."

Kyle nodded, accepting the woman's deferential manner as his due. "Thank you, Jennifer." He followed Emma into the plane, gesturing vaguely to the oversize seats. "Take your pick, honey. Ah, Jennifer?"

The flight attendant pulled out a safety seat for Chandler, which she strapped into one of the seats. Satisfied, Kyle nodded. "We'll be on the ground for a few minutes yet, Emma. If you need anything, Jennifer will see to your needs."

Emma nodded, wondering just what Jennifer thought of Kyle's passengers. She sat in the decadently comfortable leather seat facing Chandler's safety seat and leaned forward to fasten him in. Across the aisle was a long equally comfortable-looking couch.

It was silly to wish that Kyle would sit with her. But when he went through the narrow door to the cockpit and shut it securely behind him, she wished just that.

She sighed deeply, running her palms over the armrests. Jennifer moved about the cabin doing whatever it was she did.

"Mrs. Montgomery, we'll be departing momentarily."

Emma jerked her face from the window she'd been peering through. "Ah, thank you."

"You'll need to fasten your safety belt," Jennifer said gently.

"Oh." She glanced down. "Of course. I'm sorry." Then she felt her cheeks heat.

Jennifer's sleek smile suddenly took on an impish cast. "It's pretty fancy digs, isn't it?"

Emma chuckled, feeling rather uneven. She wondered what it would feel like if she really *were* Mrs. Montgomery.

The plane shuddered ever so slightly, and Emma quickly fumbled her safety belt into place. She looked over at Jennifer who sat on the end of the long couch, the picture of calm.

Emma wished she felt the same. The plane moved. She leaned forward to check on Chandler. He was working contentedly at his pacifier and Emma rested her head against the seat back and stared out the window. The takeoff was smooth as glass, and Emma finally relaxed. The landscape far below looked like a patchwork quilt.

"Chandler seems to like flying."

Emma looked up to see Kyle standing beside her seat. "Good gravy, who's flying this thing?"

"My very capable copilot. Want something to drink?"

Jennifer undid her safety belt and disappeared into a little nook near the open cockpit door.

Kyle noticed the direction of Emma's craned neck. "Want to see the action up front?"

"Well, yes, actually," she admitted.

He grinned, looking impossibly sexy despite his

conservative gray suit. With an easy motion he un-fastened her safety belt and pulled her to her feet, holding her hand as he led her to the cockpit door. It was remarkably small inside, filled with control panels and computerized-looking buttons versus the levers and knobs her mind had hazily envisioned. Kyle introduced her to his copilot, Mark Houseman, who tipped his cap and greeted her as Jennifer had done. As Mrs. Montgomery.

Kyle nudged her to the captain's seat, but Emma dug in her heels. "I couldn't. What if I bumped something?"

"There's that worrier in you coming out again."

"That's right," she agreed, and scooted past him back to her seat. Kyle joined her, accepting the steaming cup of aromatic fragrant coffee Jennifer served him in a sturdy mug—very different from the fine china that Baxter used at the house.

Emma realized that Kyle's hands looked just as comfortable wrapped around delicate English china as they did the plain white mug with the ChandlerAIR logo emblazoned on its side. Suddenly Jennifer appeared with an elegant breakfast. Frosty orange juice was in a slender crystal tumbler, and the tray holding dewy-fresh fruit and tiny pastries, which Jennifer placed on a fold-down tray near Emma's knee, was gleaming silver.

Emma couldn't resist the ripe strawberries, and she reached over and selected one, savoring its succulent sweetness. "Do all your passengers receive such five-star treatment? I imagine folks who charter this baby pay through the nose."

"This baby isn't chartered out." He leaned past

her and lifted a cluster of grapes from the tray, offering it to her first. "It's mine."

She rolled the plump green grape between her fingers. "Mine as in the company's? Or mine as in mine and you can't have it?"

Kyle chuckled. "Mine as in I share it on occasion when the need arises. But yes, mine as in I don't have to share it if I don't want to."

Emma let out a long breath. "You know, Kyle, one minute I actually let myself think you're just a regular guy, but then, this—" she waved her hand, indicating the luxuriously appointed plane "—reminds me that you're anything but ordinary. This is crazy."

"Crazy or not, we're committed to it."

"I just wish—"

Kyle touched her arm when she broke off. "Wish what?"

She shrugged, searching for the right words. "That all this wasn't necessary," she said softly. "Aside from encountering Helen Cummings, the past few weeks have been basically uneventful. I guess I let it lull me into forgetting just what we are doing." She shifted again, focusing on Chandler across from her. Watching her son was a darn sight safer than watching Kyle. "One lie leads to another, and another, each one bigger than the last."

"Do you want to turn around and go home?"

She made a face. "Right."

"I'm serious, Emma."

His voice, quiet as a sigh, was certainly serious enough. She looked at him, searching his face. "What about the Cummingses?"

"I'll figure out some plausible explanation. Tell them that you decided our brief marriage was a mistake when you found yourself married to a workaholic who put his company ahead of his family. Considering my life, it would be fairly close to the truth."

She stared at him. "You'd really turn around."

"Yes." He grimaced. "I don't want to, but I would. It's up to you, Emma. If this really is something you can't bring yourself to do, say the word. We'll turn around for Buttonwood right now."

Her chest felt tight. She had agreed to his proposition because of the financial benefit. And now she was being offered an out. She could stop it all with one simple statement. She and Chandler would go back to her cozy apartment over Penny's garage. She'd go back to work at Mom & Pop's, and while she worked, Chandler would be safely tucked in a playpen in the back office. The gossip would be ripe around Buttonwood, but it would eventually die. It always did.

One statement. A string of words that would return her and Chandler to their normal life, as if the past few weeks had never happened. As if Kyle had never been in her hospital room that first morning.

She looked down at her hands, frowning at the grape she'd squished between her fingers. Kyle slipped one of the linen napkins free from the tray and calmly wiped her fingers clean.

Except her life wasn't the same. Because she'd met Kyle Montgomery and realized she was still capable of being moved by a man, despite what Jeremy had done last summer. Not just any man, either. This man.

For that alone she knew she wouldn't back out. "No," she said softly. "We needn't turn around."

He set aside the napkin. Wrapped his hands around hers and lifted them to kiss her fingertips. "Thank you."

Jennifer stepped up to them, her expression indulgent. "Excuse me, sir. Mark says we're on the final leg."

Kyle rose. His gaze lingered on Emma. "It'll all work out, Emma. I promise you that. I don't make promises anymore I can't keep."

She nodded. He'd meant to be reassuring, she was sure. Yet she couldn't help wondering when, in his lifetime, Kyle had ever made promises he *hadn't* been able to keep.

The landing unnerved Emma only half as much as the takeoff. But it seemed that the moment the wheels of the sleek jet touched ground, every single person went into high gear. Before she knew it Kyle was holding Chandler, waiting while she climbed into the back of a long *long,* black limousine.

Then he handed the baby to her before climbing in himself. He watched her for a moment, a faint smile playing about his lips. "You haven't ridden in a limo before?"

Emma closed her slack mouth and quickly fastened Chandler into the safety seat that was waiting inside the vehicle. But when she sat back in her seat, she realized that, for all the limo's spaciousness,

Kyle still seemed a little too close for easy breath. "My drooling gave me away, I suppose."

His eyes crinkled. "It was the 'good gravy' you murmured when the driver pulled up at the plane that gave you away, I'm afraid."

Emma felt her cheeks heat. She crossed her ankles, determined not to embarrass herself any more than necessary. But she couldn't keep her eyes from roving over the luxurious interior, from the small gleaming wood bar, to the black screen of a small television, to the electronic gadgetry that controlled who knew what. "I suppose traveling this way must be very mundane for you."

He lifted one eyebrow. "I think I sense an insult in there somewhere." Yet he didn't seem the least bit offended. "Using the limo is often expedient. I can work rather than waste valuable time driving."

Emma automatically glanced at the briefcase by his feet. She'd come to realize over the past several weeks that he was rarely without it.

"In truth, I prefer to drive when I can," he finished.

"But then only if you can't fly," she said.

"You got it."

His sudden grin caught her unprepared. She was faintly aware of soft music coming from the sound system. Could barely discern the motion of the car as it built speed, leaving the airport behind. Kyle's teeth weren't quite perfect, she realized dimly. He had a minuscule chip in a front lower tooth. "You don't have caps," she said stupidly.

His eyebrows drew together. "Caps?"

She pressed her hands to her cheeks, mortified.

"Never mind." She longed to open a window, to feel the rush of air on her hot cheeks. But she wasn't even sure this thing they were riding in had windows that opened.

Kyle chuckled. "You make me laugh, Emma."

She blew out a noisy breath. "Sure. Rub it in."

His smile took on a devilish cast. "Be careful, sweetness. I might think that was an invitation."

She blinked. Then turned to face front, her whole body flushing. "And wouldn't you have a heart attack," the leading words came out without volition, "if it was."

Kyle managed to keep his smile in place. "I think we both know the fallacy of that, sweetness."

He saw her swallow hard. And he found himself wishing that no man had ever tasted that long elegant neck. His fingers slowly curled into a fist on his thigh. He'd had his secretary, Amelia, arrange the limo because he'd thought Emma would get a kick out of it. And because he could use the time to take care of some of the work he'd brought along.

He hadn't expected to sit beside Emma and think about the heavily tinted windows that afforded them tempting privacy. Or the depth of the leather seats that would accommodate them both if he should happen to pull her over to him and—

"Where's the photography studio where we're having the pictures taken?"

He shifted in the seat, reaching over to adjust the air-conditioning. "We're not going to a studio," he said. "Arrangements have been made for us at the Crest."

He was aware of the surprised look she gave him.

Extraordinarily aware of the way she turned toward him, young and vibrant and so open with her emotions it was almost painful.

"The Crest is a five-star hotel."

"Gotta sleep somewhere," he said dismissively.

Her big brown eyes widened even more.

"We'll have a two-bedroom suite," he said evenly. "A nanny will be there to help with Chandler while we say cheese for the camera. And she won't remove him from your eyesight unless you want her to. The photographer will be set up for us in the gardens."

"Won't someone see us? I mean, that was the point of going as far away as Denver to get this done, wasn't it?"

"Partly. Mostly we came to Denver, though, because the photographer I wanted couldn't make it down to Buttonwood with his schedule right now." He decided he might as well tell her now, because she was going to find out soon enough. "The photographer is one of my brothers."

She smiled, her eyes sparkling with pleasure that she would probably try to hide if she knew it was there. "How nice. Why didn't you tell me? Which brother?"

He wished he could be as certain as she that it would be nice. But at least he could be assured that news of this particular wedding shoot wouldn't make the society page. "Actually, I haven't told you about him. His name is Jake. He can be difficult," Kyle felt compelled to warn.

"Is he a lot younger than you?"

"A few years." He saw the consternation in her

eyes. "Three years," he provided. "He's thirty-six. So now you know the dirty truth. I'm looking at forty this year."

"The sight doesn't look too bad to me."

And when she looked at him from beneath her silky lashes the way she was doing now, he felt as randy as a seventeen-year-old gazing at the woman of his fantasies. He shook his head, smiling wryly, and swung his gaze to the window. The limo was just pulling up the tree-lined drive that led to the entrance of the exclusive resort. He swallowed the unease that rose in him.

He wasn't used to being so distracted by anyone or anything. Yet when he was with Emma, he was finding it increasingly difficult to remember the reason she was in his life in the first place. And finding it difficult to concentrate on the goals that had been driving him for longer than he could remember.

The car halted smoothly in front of the entrance. The chauffeur got out and opened the door for them, his expression bland while Emma climbed from the vehicle, holding Chandler against her shoulder. The long hem of her skirt dragged behind her on the carpet of the limo and Kyle felt anything but bland as one curvy calf was exposed.

He knew he had a bad case when he actually held his breath to see if Emma's skirt climbed an inch or two higher to expose the rounded curve of knee, sleek and smooth in her nylons with the pearly shine. He swallowed an oath and focused on the concierge who greeted them.

Kyle listened to the man with half an ear as he snagged the diaper bag from the bellman before it

could be taken away with their other few pieces.
Emma was doing her level best, he could tell, not to
gawk. He found her wide-eyed fascination as they
were escorted through the grand old lobby far more
charming than the concierge's obsequious commen-
tary about the hotel's amenities.

They'd reached their suite on the top floor when
Kyle had finally had enough. He took the room key
from the concierge and eyed him silently. Fortunately
the man was quick on the uptake and excused himself without delay.

Beside her Kyle unlocked the door and pushed it
open. Yet Emma couldn't quite make her feet take
that step across the threshold. She pressed her lips to
Chandler's head, nervously patting his back.

Then let out a gasp when Kyle swung her up into
her arms, Chandler and all. ''Kyle, what on earth—''

''I'm carrying you over the threshold.'' And suited
action to his words.

But rather than setting her on her feet inside the
suite, he carried her through the entry, which smelled
of the enormous bouquet of fresh summer flowers,
and into the living area of the suite. And when she
saw the beautiful grand piano standing in front of the
sparkling bay window, she couldn't help sighing with
delight.

''I thought you'd like it,'' he murmured, and carried her right over to the magnificent instrument before letting her feet find the floor. He eased Chandler
out of her arms, and Emma drew her fingers along
the spotless black finish.

Then she turned around only to find Kyle looking

down at Chandler with an expression she couldn't quite define. Yearning, maybe.

She wanted to sit at the piano and open the lid and just let her fingers rest on the keys. She wanted to watch Kyle hold her son just the way he was doing. Capably. With a hint of awe shaking his confident green gaze.

What she needed to do, however, was use the bathroom. So she excused herself, going into the bedroom that Kyle pointed toward, distracting herself for a moment with the sight of the enormous king-size bed. She shook her head at the thoughts the bed inspired. "No way, Emma."

When she reentered the living area, a uniformed maid was rolling a plastic-sheeted rack into the room, and another rosy-cheeked woman was cuddling Chandler.

Once the rolling cart was situated in the center of the room, the maid departed. Emma looked from the cart, which was nearly as tall as Kyle, to the strange person holding Chandler.

"Honey, this is Mrs. Schneider. She comes highly recommended by my sister, Sabrina."

Emma felt herself relax a little. Surely Kyle's sister's judgment was sound when it came to entrusting one's child to someone else.

"He's a beautiful boy," Mrs. Schneider said comfortably. "But a wet one, I'm afraid. So I'll just get that taken care of."

"He'll be fine," Kyle said for Emma's ears alone when the older woman took the diaper bag and went into the bedroom Emma and Chandler would use. "You need to look through the gowns and see if there's anything you like. Because if there isn't, it'll take an hour or so for the bridal shop to send over another selection. I guessed about the size, so if they're wrong, you can blame me.''

Emma's mouth ran dry as his words penetrated. She crossed to the cart and pulled away the thick black plastic to reveal a sturdy metal garment rack loaded with wedding gowns. ''Oh…my…goodness.'' They ran the gamut from slinky and sophisticated, to heavily beaded and elaborate, to puffy and ruffled. Her hands trembled as she nudged the hangers, and she quickly dropped her hands before Kyle could notice. ''Well. This is unexpected.''

''They're wedding photos, honey. What did you expect?''

She shook her head, thinking of the hours she'd spent dithering over what to wear. She knew she looked presentable. But these gowns—elaborate, expensive, impossibly beautiful—made her feel as if she was wearing sackcloth.

''You look fine just the way you are. If you prefer to wear your own clothes, say so. I'll wear a suit, instead of my tux. It'll work.''

''Don't do that. Don't read my mind.''

He pushed his hand into his pocket. ''Emma, I'm only trying to get this done without—'' He broke off, looking down for a moment. ''Without reminding you of the jerk,'' he finished flatly.

It took a moment. A long telling moment, which she'd have to examine later when her thought processes weren't muddled by Kyle's nearness. He was talking about Jeremy. He'd been thinking about the man even though Emma hadn't given him a thought at all.

It was positively liberating.

She turned to the array of gowns. There was really only one that truly tempted her. She pushed the gowns on either side of it away and pulled it from the rack, carefully easing the long skirt free from the others.

It had tiny cap sleeves, a simple scoop neck and a triple row of narrow satin ribbon circling the waist. But the skirt was like a bell-shaped cloud. She loved it on sight.

It would probably be too tight. Too long. Too something. But it was the only one she wanted to try.

She draped it carefully over her arm and turned to face Kyle. "You really brought a tux?"

He nodded once.

"Well, then, sugar, I guess you'd better go get yourself all prettied up. Because it's bad luck to see the bride in her gown before the camera flashes."

Kyle's smile was slow and sexy as sin.

And Emma's heart rolled over.

Chapter Eleven

Two hours later Kyle was pacing in the elaborate gardens the Crest laid claim to when his brother finally deigned to saunter into sight. He had a leather bag that Kyle hoped contained photographic equipment hanging from one shoulder.

Jake caught sight of him and pushed his aviator glasses down his nose to look over the rims. "Now, don't you look purty in your penguin suit."

Kyle's lips tightened. "You're late."

His brother shrugged. "Fire me." He dumped his bag on the end of a linen-draped table complete with champagne glasses and wedding cake. "Oh, that's right." Jake's mouth twisted. "You can't fire me, 'cause I'm doing you a favor."

The damnable thing was his brother was right. "Are you drunk?" Kyle demanded bluntly. Jake's eyes hadn't looked particularly bloodshot, but that didn't necessarily mean anything. Not when it came to Jake.

"If I am," his brother replied silkily, "I can still click the shutter. So where's the bride? I'll have to be sure to use filters so the dollar signs that're probably in her eyes don't show in these fool photos."

Kyle's hand curled into a fist. "You'll be nice to Emma, Jake, or I swear I'll…"

Jake shrugged out of his leather bomber jacket and dropped it carelessly on the grass. "Ground me? Cut off my allowance?" He flipped open the bag. "Don't bother. I'd just sneak out my window at night and steal some car radios to fence for money." He pulled a camera out of the bag, his smile humorless. "Oh, wait. That was you who did that stuff."

Kyle hated the reminder, even though the words were essentially true. He reminded himself that he'd come a long way from that kid and spoke calmly. "Emma hasn't done anything to deserve your disdain, Jake. So I'd appreciate it if you'd—" He sensed movement behind him. He turned and there she stood, all in white. She was…

"Exquisite," Jake said beside him.

Yes. Exquisite. More than pretty. More than striking. More than beautiful. And she took his breath away. There was nothing fancy about the dress she'd chosen. In fact, it was strikingly simple. And utterly feminine.

He barely noticed Mrs. Schneider bringing up the rear with Chandler in her arms. He had eyes only for the entrancing creature before him.

Jake stepped forward, his smile pure wolf, and

Kyle felt his gut knot. Since the death of Jake's wife five years earlier, his brother had been going out of his way to live hard, fast and furious. He was the last kind of man Emma should be exposed to.

He brushed smoothly past his brother and took Emma's hands in his. "This is Jake," he said curtly, giving his brother a hard look.

Emma wasn't sure she could find her tongue, having swallowed it at first sight of Kyle dressed in an inky-black classic tux, tailored perfectly to his wide-shouldered narrow-hipped physique. The blinding white shirt he wore made his chestnut hair look darker and his eyes even more strikingly emerald.

But good manners reared their muddled head, and she looked away from Kyle to his brother. And blinked. She immediately realized that this brother was related to Kyle by blood rather than adoption. The similarity between them was marked. But while Kyle was the epitome of strength and sophistication, Jake seemed to embody a rough earthiness. She wondered if there were more siblings Kyle hadn't mentioned.

Jake had pushed his sunglasses down his nose and was running his gaze over her from head to toe, a smile curling about his lips—lips that screamed sex and sin. She looked back at him, smiling faintly, too. Oh, he was a wild one, she was sure. And as far as she was concerned, harmless in comparison to his intense brother.

"Do I get to kiss the bride?" he asked in a husky low tone.

She tilted her head, hoping the bright sunlight didn't wilt the curls she'd coaxed into her hair before they were done with the picture-taking. "Why, of course you do." She felt Kyle stiffen beside her as she pulled her hands from his and lifted her full skirt to cross to Jake. She reached up, took his head between her hands and tugged it down to hers, then chastely tilted her cheek to him and stifled a laugh when she heard his muttered oath. But Jake kissed her cheek lightly and when Emma slid a look into his green eyes, she saw laughter there.

Then Jake looked over her head at his brother and slid his glasses back up into place. "I've got two hours to spare here, Kyle," he said abruptly, "if I'm going to be able to digitize the photos and integrate wedding guests on the computer. So let's get the show on the road."

The muscle in Kyle's jaw jumped, and Emma looked from one man to the other. Too much conflict there, she thought. She walked over to stand by Kyle and slipped her hand into his. "You can really add in people on the photographs to make it look like we had guests?" she asked Jake.

Jake nodded, his lips quirking. "We could do the whole thing without PJ there, if we put our minds to it."

Emma glanced up at Kyle. "PJ?"

He grimaced. "Forget it."

Mrs. Schneider had settled herself and Chandler off to one side under the shade of a lovely old tree. She was already burying her nose in the book she carried even as she slowly moved the carriage she'd produced back and forth. Emma had fed Chandler before dressing in the gown that had miraculously fit perfectly, and she figured he'd be quite content for the next several hours.

"At least Jake doesn't have to fabricate the wedding cake like he does guests," she murmured to Kyle. "Talk about attending to detail." She jiggled their linked hands, leaning toward him so that only he would hear. "Relax, sugar, or instead of looking like the happy bridegroom, you're going to look like you've got a shotgun pointed at your back."

Jake, apparently finished with setting out his equipment, looked up then. He'd discarded his sunglasses, and his eyes were narrowed in thought as he studied the garden setting. "Emma, love, let's get a few shots of you by the stone bench there. Do you have a veil?"

She nodded and pulled it out of the carriage where she'd stashed it, then gently shook out the long delicate tulle.

"Just hold it in your hands and look at it," he said shortly. Emma did what he requested. She tilted her chin when he said and lifted the veil when he suggested she do that so the breeze could drift through the glistening fabric.

She took the bouquet of exotic white orchids and tried to think virginal thoughts even though the sight of Kyle waiting on the sidelines sent her mind along another much more dangerous track.

The only sounds in the garden came from Mrs. Schneider, who was humming a soft lullaby to Chandler, and the whirring noise of Jake's camera.

After a long while Jake gestured for Kyle to join her. She leaned her head back against Kyle's hard chest when she was told to do so. She looked up at him when Jake said to. She even propped her satin pump on the stone bench and lifted the long skirt of her gown to reveal the lacy garter belt around her leg just above her knee.

Jake wanted Kyle to kneel at her feet and pull the garter from her knee, but Kyle hesitated, his expression unreadable. Emma put her foot back on the grass. "I need a break," she announced. She was reluctant about all this, but Kyle seemed even more so.

Kyle nodded, his lips tight. Jake shrugged and wandered over to look down at Chandler in the carriage. Emma dashed a stray curl away from her cheek and tugged Kyle down on the stone bench beside her.

"Your brother seems nice," she said after a moment.

He gave a disbelieving snort. "He detests me."

Emma turned toward Kyle, the flowing folds of her gown settling over his gleaming black boots. The man wore a tux straight out of a fashion magazine, but on his feet he wore cowboy boots. Dress boots, but boots nonetheless. "I'm sure he doesn't," she countered softly. There was a lot of strain between the two men, but Emma could honestly say she didn't believe true dislike to be part of it. "But why do you think he does?"

His lips compressed. "Well, honey, it's not a particularly pretty story. And it goes so far back I'm not sure I can even remember it all, anyway."

"Talk about a whopper," Emma murmured. But she smiled gently. "I know all about the good and bad of families. If you don't want to talk about it, I understand. Though I don't see why you never mentioned you had a natural brother.''

Kyle glanced over at Jake. "More than only a brother. I couldn't keep our family together despite my promise that I would,'' he said after a moment. "Jake blames me.''

Emma frowned. "You said you were adopted by Chandler and Lydia when you were just a teenager.''

"Yes.''

"But they didn't take Jake?''

Kyle shook his head. "We went into the foster-care system when my natural mother died,'' he said flatly. "I was twelve, Jake, nine. Trace was only seven and little Annie was five.'' He rose, tucked his hand in one pocket. "The state separated us. It took me years to find everyone again.''

Emma stood, also, her heart breaking for a young Kyle who'd tried to keep his family together despite the realities working against him. "That's hardly your fault, Kyle. You were a child.''

He shrugged. "Like I said, it's an old unattractive story.'' Again he glanced at Jake. "Let's get this wrapped up.'' He raised his voice enough for his brother to hear.

Jake nodded and sauntered back toward them. "If I recall from my misguided past, you ought to have some ceremony shots. Don't suppose there's a minister around. It'd save me some time later.''

"No,'' Kyle said, "but give me a few minutes, and I'll take care of it.'' He touched Emma's elbow gently, then strode alone down the winding path toward the hotel.

Emma gathered up her skirts and headed over to

Chandler, who wasn't the least bit impressed with her fancy dress. He far preferred sucking on his fist. Emma started to tuck the veil back in the storage area under the carriage, but Jake stopped her. "You'd be wearing the veil during the ceremony," he said.

She nodded. He was right. She wandered over to the bedecked table. The wedding cake was three tiers, all in white with elegant curls and ruffles of icing.

Jake came up beside her, stuck his finger into the icing at the base of the rear of the cake.

"You're plain wicked, aren't you," Emma said mildly.

He licked his finger, then wiped it on his worn-white blue jeans. "If Kyle is the virtuous one, then I'm the sinner," he agreed blandly. "You don't have a clue what you've gotten yourself into, do you?"

Emma looked up at the man who was so like Kyle, yet so unlike him. "Considering the tension that even an infant could detect between the two of you, I'm quite sure you don't have a clue what I've gotten myself into, either."

His eyes narrowed. Then a slow smile stretched across his mobile mouth. "Touché." But his smile died when he turned and looked at the wedding cake. "My wife would've liked this cake," he murmured.

"You're married?" She was surprised.

He slowly shook his head. "Not anymore." He abruptly turned to dig in his big battered bag.

Kyle returned with the concierge in tow. He'd even brought a Bible, and Emma swallowed the protest that immediately rose in her throat. She let Mrs.

Schneider fit the veil with its minuscule Juliet cap into place on her head. Then Jake gestured them into position, with the concierge acting as the officiant, open Bible in his hands. Emma set aside the bouquet, deliberately breathing past the breathlessness that rose in her when Kyle folded his hands around hers.

"We don't have rings." As far as she knew, Kyle hadn't done anything about that situation since their one conversation about them. Frankly she was grateful. It was one less falsehood she would have to tell on film.

Jake sighed and stepped forward, pulling a long chain out from beneath his loose black jersey. Emma barely saw the glint of diamonds and gold before Kyle lifted his hand, stopping them all. Then Jake's rings disappeared once more underneath his shirt.

Kyle reached into his pocket and pulled out two bands, one plain gold and the other glittering with a row of diamonds, opening his palm for her to see them. "I didn't forget," he said in a low voice. "But I also didn't forget your reason for not wanting to pick them out yourself."

Emma's heart pounded in her breast. How could she tell him that she hadn't been as wary of choosing wedding rings because of Jeremy as she'd been of choosing them with *him?* She plucked the larger band off his palm, curled it in her damp palm and stuck out her left hand. "Slide that little shackle into place, sugar," she drawled lightly, and pretended her hand wasn't really trembling.

Jake's camera whirred as Kyle slid the ring over her knuckle and into place on her ring finger. The band felt disturbingly comfortable on her finger. And it wasn't because she'd spent all last summer imagining Jeremy St. James's wedding band there, either. Then Emma returned the gesture, pushing Kyle's ring onto his finger.

Finally Jake lowered his camera, and Emma started to breathe easier. But he simply reloaded film and lifted it once again. "Okay, kids," he muttered. "Pucker up."

Kyle grimaced. "Dammit, Jake..."

Emma closed her hands on his forearms to keep him from saying something to his brother. "Your enthusiasm is dampening, darlin'." She smiled, even though she felt a little like kicking Jake herself.

Chandler suddenly sent up a squawk.

It seemed to jolt Kyle into action. He ran his thumb along her jaw, and just that easily, Emma blocked out the sound of Jake's camera, the way he was constantly moving around them, searching for the perfect angle, the perfect light. She forgot the concierge, who was probably damned for eternity for playing a man of the cloth in this charade.

She forgot everything but the bubble surrounding her and Kyle. Her fingertips flexed against his arms. She swallowed, her eyes falling to his lips, rising to meet his eyes. Then her lids were too heavy, and they fell as his mouth covered hers.

Indescribable pleasure sighed through her. Their lips separated for a moment and Emma heard him inhale sharply. His hands cradled her face. She slowly opened her eyes to find his gaze, hot and searching. "Kyle," she murmured, lifting her hand to touch the gleaming hair that had tumbled onto his forehead. She slowly combed through the thick strands with her fingers.

She thought she heard him say, ''I'm sorry,'' in the moment before he lowered his head once again. It was like being consumed by fire. Her head fell back and she felt his hand slide along her spine, pulling her against him.

Just where she wanted to be, she realized dimly. Her lips parted and she tasted him fully. A soft moan rose in her throat and she wrapped her arms around his shoulders, wanting to be closer, closer—

''Well. I think that pretty well melted my film,'' a voice said from somewhere.

Emma swayed weakly when Kyle lifted his head. He cupped her neck in his warm palm and pressed her head gently against his chest. ''Dammit, Jake,'' he growled.

Embarrassment came swift and hard.

She pushed out of Kyle's arms and brushed her palms down the flowing skirt of her wedding gown. Avoiding Jake, who was probably smirking, anyway, she quickly crossed to Chandler and swept him out of the carriage. He wriggled his legs and settled happily in her arms.

Reining in his irritation with his brother, Kyle thanked the concierge for his assistance. He knew the man wouldn't utter a peep about what he'd seen and done here, not with the exorbitant tip he received.

Jake switched cameras and snapped some random shots before pulling out a heavy silver pocket watch from his jeans pocket. ''I've got ten minutes to clear outta here, bud,'' he said.

Emma must have heard him, because she surrendered the baby to Mrs. Schneider and joined Kyle by the cake. She pulled off her veil and left it sitting on the end of the table out of range of the camera, then picked up one of the crystal flutes. Kyle pulled the bottle from the ice and removed the cap from the sparkling cider.

"Turning teetotaler in your old age?"

Kyle ignored Jake's mocking question and poured the sparkling golden liquid into their two flutes, then shoved the bottle back into the silver ice bucket. He picked up his flute and gently touched it to hers.

Emma smiled brilliantly, but he could see the confusion in her dark eyes.

He couldn't blame her. He was feeling a good measure of confusion himself, and he knew the reason for the undercurrents running between him and Jake. He also knew that, right or wrong, he wanted to make love to Emma.

It didn't bother him to know that Jake knew it, too. But he did feel for Emma, who was clearly unnerved by it all.

They drank the sparkling cider while Jake burned up more film. Then Emma turned to the cake and picked up the beribboned knife. When Kyle closed his hand over hers, he could feel her hand trembling. But her wide vivacious smile didn't dim a watt, and he found himself mentally applauding her.

They cut a small piece of the very real cake, and when he lifted the morsel to her mouth for her to eat, she hesitated, looking away from him. But not soon enough to hide the telltale glisten. Her throat worked for a moment, then she opened her mouth and delicately took the cake from his fingers. Her lips brushed his fingertips before she took a step back, swallowing.

His fingers tingled from that brief touch of her lips, and he stared at the bits of creamy frosting that clung to his thumb and forefinger. She was near tears and Kyle hated it. He hated having gone so far in his strategy against Cummings that he was hurting a young woman who deserved nothing of the sort.

He hated that, even knowing he was hurting her, he couldn't stop the forward momentum of the plan he'd set in motion.

She was probably thinking about the wedding she *didn't* have with the jerk who'd left her alone and pregnant. Just because Emma responded physically to Kyle didn't mean that her heart didn't still belong to that other guy.

He grabbed one of the linen napkins and wiped his fingers clean. If Emma still loved Jeremy-the-jerk, it was no business of his.

"Kyle? Don't you want your piece?"

He looked up to see Emma holding a small wedge of cake. *A piece of your heart.* The thought came out of nowhere. Unwanted. Unbidden.

He tossed down the napkin. "I think we've got enough photos by now," he said abruptly.

She didn't flinch. Didn't move. Just stood there, impossibly desirable, her slender fingers holding a morsel of cake. Everything was silent, as if the world was holding his breath.

Kyle realized he actually was. He released it just as a peal of laughter from somewhere else in the gardens drifted toward them on the breeze.

Her long lashes swept down suddenly, and she

turned toward the table, accidentally dropping the piece of cake into her champagne flute, in which a couple of inches of sparkling liquid still remained.

Just then, he felt about as appealing as that soggy piece of cake with cider bubbling and biting into it. Emma reached for a napkin, her movements uncharacteristically abrupt.

Dammit. He hadn't spent as much time feeling like an inept fool since Dennis Reid had opened Emma's hospital-room door. "Emma…"

She dropped the napkin on the table and walked away, her full skirt rustling. The sound was somehow just as accusing as the straight rigid line of her back. She stopped briefly to sweep Chandler up into her arms, and her actions seemed to scream at him not to follow her as she hurried along the winding path toward the hotel. It would be prudent to let her go, he knew.

Jake was packing up his equipment with his usual rapid thoroughness. Mrs. Schneider was brushing her palms down her clothes. Neither one seemed the least bit concerned that Emma had practically run away from their particular wedge of garden.

Kyle, on the other hand, was all too aware of it.

He yanked at the narrow bow tie strangling him and strode after her.

Chapter Twelve

Emma's flight through the luxurious lobby was interrupted by the concierge. Perhaps he thought a bride practically running through his lobby while carrying an infant was someone he needed to immediately tend. Perhaps Kyle had greased his palm so thoroughly that any sight of Kyle's party guaranteed instant personal service.

Perhaps, and more likely, she looked just this side of insane as she raced past his desk, and the safest course of action for the concierge was to make sure she made it to the suite without delay.

Whatever the man's reasons, Emma was grateful that he only handed her a keycard, escorted her to the elevator and punched the floor button for her.

Once she slammed the door of the suite behind her, however, she wished she was anywhere else than this space that she was expected to share with Kyle, no matter how platonically.

She clutched her full skirt in one hand and collapsed on one of the couches.

What a fool she was.

The gardens had been lovely with color. The wedding cake looking like something out of a magazine. And Kyle...

She was such a fool. How could she let herself get so carried away as they toasted each other with the sparkling cider? As they cut the cake?

How could she let the lines of reality and pretense blur so completely that she'd actually been living a moment that hadn't existed except in her mind?

Chandler fussed. Probably didn't like being clutched like a lifeline. She quickly wiped the tears from her eyes and took the baby into the bedroom. Once in the portable crib with his favorite blanket, he snuggled down like an angel and slept.

If only she could press her cheek to a pillow and sleep away all that was wrong. Too agitated to remain in the bedroom with Chandler, she went out into the living area. The piano drew her like a magnet and the gown swished around her feet when she perched sideways on the bench.

Her eyes burned as she stared down at the gown. The style hadn't been particularly formal, but she'd still let herself feel like Cinderella at the ball.

Except her Prince Charming didn't come calling with glass slipper in hand and words of love and forever on his lips. He flew a plane and worked too hard and believed that the end justified the means.

She bent forward, propping her forehead in her

hands. A hot tear burned its way down from her tightly closed eyes. "I knew he was trouble," she muttered. "But did I pay attention? No, of course not. That would've been too smart. Too sensible."

She wiped her cheeks and lifted her head. She couldn't even be angry with Kyle. For what had *he* done? Been generous with his home? Offered security for Chandler that she could've spent years trying and failing to achieve? Shown her that she wasn't dead inside, the way she'd thought, after being betrayed by Jeremy and the rest of the St. James family?

She sniffed and swung around on the piano bench, automatically lifting the lid. She·stroked the surface of the keys with her fingertips.

When had she begun falling for him?

Had it been when he'd brought her warm blueberry pie with ice cream melting all over it? When he'd walked Chandler to sleep that one night?

Perhaps it had been the day he'd shocked Flo and Blanche by telling them she was his wife.

Or maybe it had been that very first day. When he'd looked at her with his mesmerizing green eyes and said he was looking for a wife.

It didn't matter when. It just was. And if she'd been unsuitable for the St. James family, she was *really* unsuitable for the position of Mrs. Kyle Montgomery.

Taking a shuddering breath, she found the only solace there was just then. Playing the piano.

Kyle heard the haunting notes as soon as he opened the door to the suite. The sight of Emma, her head bent over the piano as she drew a painfully bittersweet tune from the instrument, was unobstructed from where he stood.

He closed the door quietly, but it wouldn't have mattered if he'd made more noise. She was lost in the music.

He could see it in the angle of her head, in the vulnerable curve of her neck. In the fingers that seemed to become part of the piano, making it a part of herself.

God, did she weep inside the way the music wept?

He crossed the room. "Emma."

Her shoulders stiffened and she pulled her hands off the keys as if she'd been caught with her fingers in the cookie jar. She pressed her hands to her lap until they disappeared among the fluffy white stuff of her wedding gown. "Has your brother gone?"

"Probably." Kyle didn't want to talk about Jake.

"What does he do?" she asked after a moment.

"Keeps everyone and everything at a comfortable distance."

"He's like you, then."

Kyle frowned, but couldn't quite deny it. "Perhaps." He pressed his thumb against the underside of the unfamiliar gold band he wore. "Tell me about Chandler's father."

He heard her audible intake of breath. "What for?"

He waited a few moments before responding. He didn't want to make yet another false step. Blunder more than he already had. He didn't want to be the reason she played such sad notes on the piano.

He didn't want the memory of an old love to be the reason, either.

"You were in love with him."

She slowly replaced the lid over the keys, and his body tightened at the way her fingers lingered over the gleaming black finish. "I thought so," she admitted after a moment.

"Where did it go wrong?"

Her lips twisted. "He didn't love me."

Kyle found that hard to believe. "He said that?"

"He didn't have to. He already had a fiancée. Who wasn't yours truly. That made it pretty clear."

If he'd only heard her dry tone, he might have believed that her heart hadn't been wounded by the jerk's actions. But he saw her face. Saw the wounds that hadn't yet healed. "His being engaged to someone else doesn't necessarily mean he didn't love you." Kyle made himself say the words, for they were true even if he found them unpalatable.

"Well, it's all water under the bridge now. Last I heard, the wedding is expected to be the summer's society event for Colorado Springs."

"He comes from money," Kyle murmured.

She nodded, her palm slowly caressing the surface of the piano.

"And his family didn't approve of the music student for a wife."

Emma stiffened, looking up at him with surprise. Then her soft mouth turned down at the corners, and her cheeks flushed. "I guess it's not a particularly original story. But I suspect it was my Tennessee background they found particularly embarrassing.

Goodness knows they spent enough time investigating what they termed my welfare roots.''

"It's their embarrassment, Emma. Not yours. You didn't do anything wrong.''

She pressed her palms flat on the curved keyboard cover. "Are you so sure?''

Her voice was low and he could barely hear the question. "Yes," he said quietly. "I am sure.''

She was silent for a moment. Then she looked at him, her eyes dark and so full of emotion that his gut ached. She moistened her lips. "Thank you.''

Their eyes held for a moment that stretched a little too long for comfort. Kyle's comfort, anyway. "I'm hungry," he announced abruptly. "Think you can trust Mrs. Schneider long enough with Chandler to join me for dinner?''

"Oh, I don't... Is she still here?''

Kyle was glad she hadn't completed her immediate objection. "I arranged lodging for her here, too.'' He hadn't allowed for a single thing to interfere with his plans to get their wedding album under way. "We can have dinner right here at the Crest. There are a couple of restaurants.'' He held out his hands, palms up. "It's been a long day, Emma, and we might as well have a nice dinner. What do you say?''

"I'll need to change first.''

"Take as long as you need.'' He smiled slightly. "I'm starving, but I guess I can wait a little longer.''

"Ah, no—'' her cheeks went pink ''—that's not what I meant.'' She rose, smoothing her graceful hands down the folds of her sweeping dress. "The gown,'' she said. "I, well, I can't reach the buttons. Mrs. Schneider helped me earlier.'' She turned, showing him her back and the long line of tiny round pearls that ran from the base of her neck to below her hips.

"He curled his fingers. "I'll get Mrs. Schneider."

"Oh." She didn't look at him. "Actually, if you could just, ah, undo the top few, I can get changed while you make sure she can watch Chandler. It'll save a little time, since you said you were really hungry."

"Starving," he murmured. He uncurled his fists and stood, walking up behind her, nudging his boots under the folds of the gown so he didn't damage the fabric. He smoothed her shiny hair away from the nape of her neck, exposing the top buttons.

She reached up and held her curls out of his way.

Kyle's jaw tightened and he reached for the first button. His pulse roared in his ears and his fingers felt too big and clumsy as he tried to slip the round little button through the narrow loop.

"There's a hook at the top," she said.

He looked. Unfastened it and then managed to unfasten the top one. And the second. And the third. Her skin was pale and smooth as dairy cream. The fourth. The fifth. Her shoulder blade where a tiny mole taunted him, sassy and sexy as hell. The sixth. The lacy edge of a corset-looking thing. The seventh. Eighth.

The little cap sleeves slid forward from her slender shoulders, and Emma lifted her hands to hold the gown against her breasts.

He drew in a long breath. More buttons. Her corset was clearly visible now, hugging her slender back. Her narrow waist. The seductive flare of hip. He worked free another button, his knuckles grazing the slick fabric that molded her skin. He went still for an agonizing moment. Then moved his hands from temptation and stepped away. "There're still some buttons left, but it looks like you can—"

"Yes," she said quickly, turning, holding the dress up, avoiding his eyes. "It's fine, Kyle. Thank you." With her free hand, she gathered up a fist of skirt and headed for her bedroom.

Close the door, Emma, he commanded silently.

She looked back at him as if she'd heard his thoughts. She let go of her skirt and slowly closed the door, hiding her creamy skin and satin-clad curves from view.

Kyle blew out a long breath and yanked at the studs on his shirt.

"Kyle?" Emma peeked at him from behind the door, but he could see her bare shoulder.

Torturing himself wondering what else was bare, he shoved his hands into his pockets. "Yes?"

"I should probably wear the outfit I came in rather than jeans, right?"

Jeans. Snug ones that hugged her hips and outlined her legs. Which Baxter had delighted in describing a time or two, but which Kyle had not had the pleasure to witness himself. He'd been too busy at ChandlerAIR. Too busy with finding one reason after another to stay away from his house.

Or the classy number she'd worn on the plane. Either one was fine with him.

Nothing at all was fine with him.

"The skirt and jacket," he suggested gruffly. "That'll be more than fine for the dining room."

She nodded and softly closed the door.

Kyle raked his fingers through his hair. He couldn't believe he'd been stupid enough to think he could keep things strictly business where Emma was concerned.

Subdued lighting, soft music, lowered voices. Linen tablecloths, heavy silver and gleaming crystal. That was Emma's hazy impression of the dining room at the Crest. Despite the fact that it was summer, a fire flickered in an enormous stone fireplace across the room. Yet it didn't seem to add undue heat.

Every table was placed for optimum privacy, and the waiters anticipated the needs of their patrons almost before the diners were aware of any.

What Emma was most conscious of, however, was not the elegant décor, the intimate atmosphere, the impeccable service or the perfectly prepared meal. It was the man seated across from her. The man who'd turned her world on end from the moment he'd entered her hospital room that fateful day.

The man who had turned the simple task of undoing a few buttons into a wholly sensual experience, which still had her nerve endings jangling.

"How's the dessert?"

She looked down at the fluffy concoction of cream and kiwi and ten other things that the waiter had described but that Emma couldn't recall. "Delicious." She set down her dessert fork, though. "But I'm afraid if I eat another bite, I'll burst a seam."

His eyes crinkled. "That might be an interesting sight."

Emma smiled and shook her head. It was safer looking around at the other diners than at him, so she did. "Have you been here before?"

"Once."

"With a beautiful sophisticated woman on your arm, no doubt," she said lightly.

His lips twitched. "I'm sure my sister Sabrina would appreciate the description. I brought her here for her twenty-fifth birthday."

Emma absently rotated the stem of her water goblet between her thumb and forefinger. "She lives in Denver, too?"

"Yes. So do Bolt and Trev and Felicia when she's not traveling around the state. Gillian is in Europe with her ballet company."

"My goodness. How exciting."

"Grueling, actually. At least that's what she said in her last letter."

Emma propped her elbow on the table and rested her chin in her palm, looking right at him, because no matter how hard she tried, she couldn't help it. Her gaze just naturally wanted to rest on him. "You keep up with them all, don't you? I admire that. The perfect big brother."

His lips twisted. "Jake would disagree."

"You said you've reconnected with your other birth brothers and sisters?"

He nodded.

"And they all know one another, as well? Your birth family and your adoptive family?"

"No. Let's dance."

Emma blinked, sitting up straighter. Looked beyond his shoulder to the small dance floor where a few couples were lazily circling in time to the strains of a lone guitar. What an appealing idea. But she knew that the idea of holding her in his arms wasn't what prompted his abrupt suggestion.

"You know, Kyle," she said softly, "sometimes talking about the past helps put it to rest."

"And sometimes, Emma, talking about the past leads only to *un*rest."

"In other words, don't ask you why Jake called you PJ?"

He looked at her, then shook his head and smiled wryly. "Yeah."

She smiled, too. It was hard not to when he was this way. Relaxed—at least as relaxed as she'd seen him, his remarkable eyes glinting with humor. "If you have brothers and sisters living right here in Denver, why are you staying at the Crest? Having dinner with me? Don't you want to see them while you're in town?"

"I'd just as soon they not get too big a whiff of what I'm doing."

"Having fake wedding photos created, pretending to be married, you mean?" She pulled her elbow from the table and folded her hands in her lap. "You don't want to lie to your family, but it's okay to lie to Mr. Cummings. To my friends in Buttonwood."

"Emma."

Sharp disappointment was coursing through her, and no matter how badly she'd like to be sophisticated and capable, she couldn't. "That's not an accurate take on the situation?"

"I don't want the rest of my family to know what

I'm doing because word would get back to my adoptive parents about the deal with Cummings.''

"So?"

"So they'd try to stop me. And I won't be stopped. Not about this. Not when I'm so close.''

"But why? You said yourself that it's good business sense for ChandlerAIR. And if Mr. Cummings wants the deal, as well, what could your parents possibly object to?'' If he could only explain it to her so she'd understand, then perhaps she could justify her foolish fascination for him.

Kyle just shook his head, then subtly motioned for the check. Emma sat back, sighing. So much for the lovely dinner they'd just shared. All because she couldn't keep her tongue under control. She looked at the dance floor, wishing she'd had the nerve to dance with him when he'd suggested it. "You're a complicated man.'' She'd thought as much before.

The waiter appeared silently beside Kyle, then disappeared just as silently after Kyle had scrawled his name on the check. Kyle looked at Emma, one brow raised slightly. "Not really. I have a goal and I don't want any more hitches in the plan to achieve it than necessary.''

"And my pretending to be your wife is all part of the plan.''

"Essentially.'' He rose and held out his hand to her. "Except you've thrown a few unexpected hairpin turns in the road.''

Emma looked at his hand. Long blunt fingers. Wide square palm. He had hard little pads of callus that she wouldn't have expected from a man who was the employer rather than the laborer. "Hairpin turns? I can't imagine what you mean."

He wrapped those long blunt fingers around her wrist and pulled her to her feet. "You know, sweetness," he murmured. "You know damned good and well what I mean. You have a tiny little mole on your shoulder blade," he said for her ears alone.

"I know." She tugged her hand from his. "Chandler is probably hungry by now."

"Right here," he continued, as if she hadn't spoken. They walked through the quiet lobby toward the elevator and he pressed his palm against her shoulder blade. It seemed to burn right through her jacket to her flesh. "I'm going to be thinking about that tempting little spot for the rest of my days. Wondering if your skin is as soft as it is creamy. If it's as sweet as the honey that flows in your voice."

And now she'd be thinking about his lips on her shoulder blade, too.

But nothing had changed between them. Not really. He might be able to send her from amusement to hurt to heaven within the blink of an eye. But Kyle still believed the end justified the means. And he'd made his priorities perfectly clear. His business came first with him.

It always would.

Chapter Thirteen

Chandler was crying.

It was nearly two in the morning, and Kyle was still sprawled on the couch in the living area of the suite, where he'd been since Emma had gone to bed hours earlier. Still staring at the television screen.

He didn't want to listen to the television any more than he wanted to listen to the voice inside him that kept insisting he was heading down the wrong path.

He picked up the tumbler of scotch he'd been nursing since midnight and stared into the liquid. He wasn't much of a drinker. The booze only reminded him of his first mother, Sally, and as such had about as much appeal as swallowing glass shards.

Chandler continued crying.

It would be risky to go into Emma's bedroom, though. Particularly after the day they'd had. His resistance was shot to hell. Emma was still recovering from the jerk. It was a combination that spelled disaster.

He could too easily take advantage of Emma's generous spirit. God, he already was. Using her need to provide for her son in order to obtain her help in closing the deal on CCS. Kyle didn't want to hurt her even more. He couldn't give Emma what she deserved any more than the jerk had.

Families and forever were for the young and idealistic. Kyle was neither. He was thirty-nine and a little too jaded and a lot too committed to his work to even think about starting out on that life course.

Yet still he wanted Emma. Wanted to run his fingers along her lovely cheek. Wanted to see her shiny dark hair spread across his white pillowcase. Wanted to draw her floaty feminine skirt slowly up from her ankles, over her curvy calves and above her knees…

With an oath Kyle set the glass on the cocktail table. Thinking that way would only ensure he'd spend the rest of the night as sleepless as he was now.

Chandler's crying had grown more fretful. He rose and crossed to Emma's closed door. Pressed his palm against the wood and told himself he wasn't going in there.

He could hear Chandler's pitiful wails. Hiccuping, brokenhearted.

Suddenly the door opened right beneath his hand, and Emma stood there, Chandler pressed to her shoulder. She gasped, backing up a step. "Kyle."

Her eyes were dark and worried. "What's wrong?" he asked.

"I think he's sick," she said miserably. "He feels hot and he…he won't nurse, and I know he must be hungry."

Kyle reached out and cupped his hand around Chandler's head. His neck was warm, but then, weren't most babies' squirmy little bodies warm? He held out his other hand and took the baby from her. "Are you sure he's hungry? Maybe he just doesn't like the unfamiliar surroundings."

He looked at Emma, who nibbled her lip and glanced away from him. She waved her hand vaguely. "I just know."

Kyle lifted a brow. "This is one of those mother-child nonverbal things?"

She flushed. Pressed her fingertips to the hollow in her throat. "My milk," she whispered. "I…"

Kyle couldn't help it. He was a slug, but he was a male slug. He looked at her breasts, pushing against the oversize tomato-red nightshirt that hung off one slender shoulder and fell past her knees. He turned away, striding to the telephone. Chandler *did* feel warm.

"What are you doing?"

"Calling the concierge. He can round up a doctor to come and check on Chandler."

She followed him, her arms folded protectively across her chest. To ease her need to nurse or to hide from his eyes? He almost told her not to bother. She could wear stinking wet burlap and he'd still feel compelled to look.

"They can really do that?" She looked relieved and surprised all at once and Kyle nodded, impulsively putting his hand behind her neck. The kiss he pressed to her forehead was for him as much as for her, he realized. "Thank you. I'm sure it's probably nothing, but…"

"You'll feel better knowing for sure."

She brushed her hair away from her face. "Yes."

Kyle's gut tightened. Her eyes darkened. The moment lengthened.

Then she deliberately moved away, putting the width of a couch between them. "I guess you're mighty used to figuring a woman's mind." Her drawl was smooth.

"Just yours, honey."

She rolled her eyes and turned toward the piano, and he let it pass. What good would it do to let her know how easily she'd gotten under his skin? How her feelings were transmitted so easily to him?

Chandler seized that moment to tangle his little fingers in the hair on Kyle's chest, and Kyle gingerly removed the baby's grip. At least he'd stopped crying so hard, only shuddering now and then with a sad little sob. "I get the message," he murmured. "Protecting your mama again."

He picked up the phone and dialed. Within minutes he was assured that a physician was on his way. He hung up and turned to see Emma sitting sideways on the piano bench. She'd drawn up her knees and pulled the stretchy shirt over her knees until all he could see were the pink tips of her toes. "Play if it'll make you feel better," he suggested.

She looked at the instrument beside her. "I'd be afraid of disturbing one of the other guests," she murmured. "It's awfully late." Her gaze followed him as he slowly walked Chandler around the suite.

"Kyle?" She hesitated for a moment, then decided to ask. "Why haven't you ever married? Had kids of your own?" She suddenly frowned. "Or have you been? I mean, I just assumed—"

"Never had time." He cut off her flustered words.

"You're a natural with kids. Look at Chandler. He's practically asleep again, and it's because of you." Her face went pink. "I know it's none of my business."

Sure enough. The baby's eyes were closed, the picture of innocence. "When I was younger," he found himself admitting, "I always said that marriage and kids could come later. That I wanted to get the business fully established before I concentrated on my personal life."

"Sugar, I don't know how you define *established,* but it looks to me like ChandlerAIR's pretty well grown-up."

He smiled faintly. "Yeah. I guess the real reason I kept putting off having a family of my own was that I didn't want to be the miserable failure at it that my father was. My birth father," he elaborated. And admitting it seemed ridiculously simple.

Because she was a good listener? Because she had her own share of demons to struggle with? Or just because she had a voice like warm honey and melting brown eyes a man could get lost in?

"Jake had a twin," he found himself telling her. "Janice. She drowned in our swimming pool when she was two. I think my...father blamed my mother."

"Oh, Kyle. How terrible for your family. Your mother must have been devastated."

"If she was, she kept it buried under pills and booze." He wished he'd kept the bitter words unsaid when Emma's eyes suddenly glistened. "She held it together for a while," he allowed. "Eventually, though, the old man decided the family he had left wasn't worth his time, and he took off a few years after the accident. She pretty well fell apart after that."

"My daddy left, too," she murmured. Then smiled sadly. "Stinks, doesn't it?"

Amusement, faint though it was, where there had only been bitterness whenever he thought of his father, rolled through him. "Yeah," he agreed. "It stinks."

"You wouldn't do that to your family."

"How do you know?"

She gazed at him. "I just do. Look at the way you found your sister and brothers when you were separated after your mama died. And the way you talk about Sabrina and your adoptive family now." She pushed her feet out from under the nightshirt and stood. "But don't worry, Kyle. I won't tell anyone that under that power suit and tie of yours resides a closet family man. Your secret is safe."

The knock on the door precluded his having to respond. Which was just as well, because if she knew the thoughts swirling in his head whenever he looked at her, she wouldn't be worrying about the safety of his secrets. She'd be worrying about how to fend off a man whose good intentions had been eroded under the onslaught of the desire she aroused in him.

Emma hurried to the door and flung it open, reminding Kyle forcibly that she was entirely too trusting. But it was the doctor, and after handing over her business card, the woman quickly examined Chandler. Being wakened, however, pleased the baby not at all and within minutes, he let everyone within earshot know it.

Emma sat on the couch beside the doctor, trying to comfort Chandler. She recounted the past few days, trying to explain his fussiness, but felt helpless to come up with a real reason. The doctor listened, nodding. "I imagine this is a reaction to the inoculation you mentioned. Babies sometimes experience discomfort after receiving vaccines."

"Discomfort," Emma muttered. "There's that word again. I didn't even think of that."

The doctor smiled sympathetically as she wrote on a pad. Then she tore off the scrawled instructions and handed them, along with a small bottle of infant acetaminophen, to Emma. "If he's not feeling his usual self by tomorrow, give your regular pediatrician a call. But truly, I think your son will be fine very soon. And if he doesn't want to take the breast, express as you need to so that you're not uncomfortable and keep it in the fridge. He'll probably make up for his lack of hunger with a vengeance later."

Emma gathered Chandler against her shoulder, feeling her cheeks heat because Kyle was standing right there and had heard every word. It was juvenile, she knew. And if he were anybody else, she wouldn't feel so conscious of the very natural functions of her body.

She just couldn't help it. The thoughts she had of Kyle were not *remotely* maternal. With each passing minute in his presence she only became more aware of her femininity. So acting blasé about breast feeding with him so close by, his white shirt hanging, unbuttoned and sexily rumpled to expose a chest that was most definitely male, most definitely mature and most definitely the finest chest she'd ever seen, was simply beyond her ability.

She realized the doctor was at the door, and Emma flushed even more as she rose to thank the woman for coming at such an hour.

Then she turned to face Kyle. Kyle who didn't have on his regulation tie, whose sharply carved jaw was blurred with a sexy shadow of whiskers, and whose rigid abdomen drew her traitorous attention like a magnet. Kyle, whose words about exploring the small mole on her shoulder blade had been tormenting her since he'd delivered them.

She snatched up the bottle of pain reliever the doctor had left. "Thank you for getting the doctor. I appreciate it."

"I wanted to make sure he was fine, too."

"I believe you." As far as she could tell, he hadn't been dishonest about a single thing.

Except pretending that they were wed.

She stifled a sigh and held up the little bottle. "Well, I guess we'll go back to bed. I'm sorry we woke you."

"You didn't." He shoved one hand through his hair and sat on the couch, picking up the drink that was still sitting there. He propped one boot on the edge of the cocktail table and leaned back, resting the squat glass on his hard bare stomach. He dropped his head against the couch and closed his eyes. "Go to bed, Emma."

She curled her bare toes into the plush carpet, wanting to say something more, but not knowing what.

Stifling a sigh, she carried Chandler into the bedroom. Then she coaxed a few drops of sticky red liquid into his mouth and settled him in the portable crib the hotel had provided where he miraculously closed his eyes with a little sigh and went to sleep.

Emma wearily climbed back into the enormous lonely bed and tucked a pillow under her cheek. But sleep didn't come to her the way it had to Chandler.

She turned onto her other side, looking at the faint line of light at the bottom edge of the closed bedroom door. She didn't know how long she lay there, waiting for that light to go out. For the sound of another door closing. Anything to indicate that Kyle had gone to bed.

Nothing. The light remained.

She pressed an arm over her eyes, but she couldn't blot out the vision of him, sprawled on the couch, a tumbler of amber liquid propped on his stomach.

She pushed herself up on her elbows, staring at the door. Beside the bed, she could hear the soft cadence of Chandler's breath. In her head, she could hear the thump of her own heartbeat.

She blew out a long breath. Pushed back the blankets and climbed out of bed. Kyle looked up from his position on the couch when she opened the door.

"Chandler?"

Emma shook her head, quietly closing the door behind her before walking toward the couch. "He's sleeping, thank goodness." Her nerve took her as far as the arm of the couch and she lowered her hip onto it, self-consciously smoothing the nightshirt over her knees.

"So why aren't you sleeping, too?"

She lifted one shoulder. "You aren't."

He smiled, but it was grim. Either he'd refilled the tumbler he still held or he hadn't had so much as a sip.

"Why *aren't* you?" She slipped from the arm to the couch, curling her legs up on the cushion beside her. "Sleeping, that is."

He looked at her and heat swirled through her chest just that quickly. That easily.

That frighteningly.

He sighed, took a grimacing sip of his drink before setting it down and stole her breath when he wrapped one warm hand around her ankle. "Talk to me, Emma." His voice was low. Husky. Made her skin tingle. Or maybe that was because of the thumb he was rubbing back and forth over the sensitive spot behind her ankle.

"About what?" she asked.

He shook his head slightly. "Doesn't matter. Anything." A slice of sharp green looked her way, then he closed his eyes and dropped his head against the cushion. "Talk to me, honey, or we're gonna get into trouble here, no matter what kind of intentions we've got."

Emma swallowed, unable to find words. But Kyle's warm hand slid up her calf, nudged beneath the baggy hem of her nightshirt and cupped her knee. Her lips parted. The only word she could form was his name, which emerged like a squeak. She moistened her lips, agonizingly aware of Kyle's fingers slowly caressing her knee. "Is Jake usually a wedding photographer?" she asked desperately.

"No. He was a photojournalist."

"Was?"

"Before his wife died. Were you a virgin when you met the jerk?"

Emma blinked. The nightshirt crept up to her knee as Kyle's fingertips brushed the outer curve of her thigh. "I...yes." Her eyes closed for a moment and she let out a long shaky breath. "Not that it's any of your business," she felt compelled to add.

"First time I slept with a girl I was fourteen. She was nineteen. She rented a room in one of the foster homes I'd been stuck with. I didn't get to stay there long, needless to say."

"Were there a lot of foster homes?"

He smiled faintly. "That's all you have to ask? Nothing more about my sexual precociousness?"

She pressed her hand over his. Separated only by the material of her shirt, but keeping his long fingers from creeping any higher. He was halfway up her thigh. Much farther and she was going to go out of her mind. "Were there?"

"Five."

"What about Jake and...Trace, right? And little Annie. Where did they go? Wasn't there any attempt to keep you all together?"

"I was one step from being a juvenile delinquent," he said evenly. "We were deliberately separated so that I couldn't continue being a bad influence on them. Annie was younger. She was adopted almost immediately, but the family moved around a lot. Trace lucked out a bit, too. He ended up in a group home in Wyoming on some children's ranch. He's still there. Helps run the place now. Jake…well, you've met him.''

''I can't see you as a juvenile delinquent.''

His lips twisted. ''Doesn't fit with the suit?''

''Doesn't fit with your…oh, code, I guess. You're too ethical.''

''Considering how you feel about our make-believe marriage, I'm surprised you credit me with ethics at all. But ethics didn't buy food for my sister and brothers. And the car radios I got busted for stealing did.''

''My mother never had money, either.''

''Sally had money,'' Kyle said. ''She just blew it on other things.''

From the bits and pieces Kyle had imparted, Emma could just imagine what those other things had been, and her heart broke for that long-ago family that had borne more than its share of tragedy. It surprised her not at all that Kyle had turned to whatever means he'd felt he needed to in order to provide for his brothers and sister. ''Why wasn't some attempt made by the authorities to find your father when your mama died?''

''There was.'' With the ease of long practice, Kyle kept the dark anger inside him from rearing its head. ''He didn't want us before Sally died. He didn't want us after.''

Emma shifted on the couch beside him, leaning toward him. Soft and warm. Strong and healthy. ''But then you and the Montgomerys found one another. You moved on. And look at you now. Successful. Respected. You've put the bad stuff behind you."

Her earnestness moved him more than he wanted to acknowledge. "I'll bet your personal motto is that one about life giving you lemons, so you make lemonade."

"What if it is? It's yours too, even if you haven't realized it."

He nearly laughed. "Honey, trust me. That isn't my motto."

"A rose is a rose," she insisted, pushing one hand through her hair, tucking it behind her ear. "Your home life with your first family was less than ideal, but you didn't cut yourself off from them. You reconnected with them when you had an opportunity to. And now you employ hundreds of people at ChandlerAIR, employees whose loyalty you have because of your progressive employee relations. Gracious, you've won business awards and all sorts of things, even."

He raised an eyebrow.

"I've been reading up on you," she said, then blushed. "I mean on ChandlerAIR, of course."

"I liked the first version better."

She pressed her lips together for a moment. "Anyway, I…"

He waited. "You…?"

"Forgot what I was going to say," she whispered.

He felt her gaze on his lips, and the simmering heat inside him instantly shot to full boil. "Emma."

She sucked in her lower lip for a moment, leaving it with a glisten that cranked up the flame inside him even more. He slipped his hands easily around her waist and pulled her right across his lap, anchoring her hips shockingly against his. "Talking isn't working anymore," he said, and swallowed her gasp with his lips.

Don't ever stop.

The plea ran silently through Emma's whirling mind. Kyle's hands burned through her nightshirt, and she curled her fingers against his shoulders.

His kiss devoured. Teased. Seduced. And his hands, oh, his hands shaped her back. Drifted along her spine, making her shiver, arch against him. Wish frantically that there wasn't so much fabric separating them.

Don't ever stop.

An involuntary moan rose in her throat when he lifted his mouth from hers. There was no hesitation in his heavy-lidded gaze. He curled his fingers in the bunched hem of her nightshirt. Yet Emma knew she could halt this heavenly madness now.

She caught the tip of her tongue between her teeth and raised herself ever so slightly onto her knees. The nightshirt slid upward. Cool air. Then heat when his hands followed the upward ascent of the material. Her breath shuddered through her. Her pulse deafened her.

She slowly lifted her arms. Up. Off.

His long fingers captured her wrists, gently anchoring them at her sides, and his eyes burned over her, making her flesh tighten. She wished with the one brain cell that was still functioning that she was wearing more seductive panties than her plain white cotton. "Kyle."

"Shh." His warm palms slid over her hips, run-

ning along the hem of her unimaginative panties with
such thoroughness that she forgot what was wrong
with them in the first place. She forgot everything
except him when his palms glided along her back,
cradling her weight as he slowly lowered his head to
one aching peak. "You're beautiful," he murmured,
then touched his tongue to her.

She sucked in her breath, her very soul quaking.
One tiny little touch, exquisite in its deliberate goal.
She caught her hands in his thick chestnut hair and
tugged, blindly pressing her lips to his. Mindlessly
fitting her soft curves against him.

She opened her mouth to him, pushed her hands
beneath the sides of his shirt and reveled in the feel
of hard bunching muscle sprinkled with intriguing
swirls of hair. But even that wasn't enough, and she
tugged the fine fabric off his shoulders. He released
her long enough to yank his arms out of the rolled-
up sleeves. Emma trembled wildly, sinking her teeth
into her lower lip as their frenzy was suspended for
a taut moment.

Kyle closed his hands over her shoulders. Slowly
drew them along the sides of her breasts. Down her
rib cage. Her hips. She opened her mouth for breath.
"Don't ever stop," she whispered.

A muscle worked in his jaw. Then he put his hands
high on her thighs and pulled her tightly against him.
Her head fell weakly forward to his shoulder and she
sank helplessly against him as convulsions swept
through her with lightning speed.

"Ah, sweetness," he breathed against her forehead, his hands on her hips guiding, urging.

Holding her safe when she finally stopped quaking

and could only cling to him, heart racing, eyes burning.

His fingers threaded through her hair, and he looked into her face. "You're beautiful," he said softly, thumbing away a tear from her cheek. "I've never wanted a woman more than I want you right now."

She simply had no words. She pressed her lips to his. And held on, when he pushed them both from the couch and carried her into his bedroom.

He settled her in the middle of the bed, and Emma drank in the sight of him, standing there so masculine. So sure. He was more than beautiful, she thought faintly. She knew a man could be handsome on the outside and empty on the inside. But Kyle wasn't like that.

He was determined and responsible and, despite the marriage charade they were playing, honorable to the core.

She pushed up on one arm and reached for him. But he caught her hands and shook his head. "I don't have anything with me," he said evenly.

She blinked. Then realized. Her mouth rounded in a silent *Oh*.

He smiled slightly. "Your disappointment flatters me." He let go of her hand and sat on the bed, leaning over to yank off his boots and socks. Then he stretched out beside her, sliding away her panties in one sure stroke. She stilled his hands. "Kyle, I want to, but…but we can't."

His smile was slow, decidedly wicked and filled with promise. "There're dozens of ways, Emma," he reminded her.

Emma's heart seemed to stutter. He smoothed his palms along her thighs. "Mercy," she said.

He chuckled softly and drew his fingertips enticingly along her knees, parting them ever so sweetly. "Did I ever tell you that I've got a thing for your knees?"

Emma couldn't answer to save her soul. She was too busy climbing to the stars.

Chapter Fourteen

"Stop fidgeting."

"I'm not." Emma let her hands fall to her sides to prove it. But not two seconds passed before she touched the locket at her throat to make sure she'd fastened the necklace correctly.

Kyle shut the car door and caught her hand in his. "You are."

She sighed and shifted on the sidewalk. "I don't want to mess this up for you," she admitted. They were two minutes away from entering the Cummingses' home. In Kyle's hand was the photo album, delivered by courier to his place that very morning.

Jake had done his job well. The photographs showed a beautiful wedding, a beautiful setting, laughing, smiling guests and a bride and groom who appeared to be totally in love.

In Emma's case that last was all too true.

"Are you sure Baxter doesn't mind keeping Chandler for us while we're gone?"

Kyle lifted a brow. "Emma."

She shrugged, knowing how ridiculous the question had been. She couldn't help it. She was as nervous as a cat. "I'm not a good actress," she reminded him.

"Relax. You're not going to be put on a witness stand. Look at all the cars lining the street here. There's probably two dozen people in that house."

Emma nodded. "I know that. I just...well, sugar, you're tense, too." His hands were tight on the thick album and a muscle jumped in his jaw. She could handle her own nervousness. But knowing that Kyle wasn't entirely certain about the evening completely unnerved her. "We should have come up with some excuse to cancel."

"There's no time to cancel," he said. "The final contracts to acquire CCS are ready. Cummings just needs to sign on the dotted line."

Emma shouldn't have been surprised. It was the whole point of this make-believe marriage. But the dagger-sharp pang of dismay she felt at the news was all too real. Once the deal was done, her presence in Kyle's life would no longer be necessary. She swallowed past the lump in her throat. "You must be happy about that."

"Yes."

He didn't look happy. He looked...tense. There was simply no other word for it.

"Is there any chance that Mr. Cummings might back out?"

"There's always a chance. It's unlikely, though."

"And after the dotted line is signed, then what?"

"Then I'll have everything I want," he murmured.

Emma looked down at her hands. Of course. Kyle had never made any bones about the priorities in his life. And ChandlerAIR was the number-one priority. She took a breath and let it out, turning to face the Cummingses' pillared house. "Baxter told me he'd been married," she said as they started walking toward it. "Back when he was a mechanic."

"So you asked him about that."

"This morning." She stared blindly at the neatly groomed shrubbery lining the walk. "He says he put his career before his wife, and when she left him, he took it badly. Started drinking too much. Nearly caused a terrible plane accident because of it."

"He never drank again, never worked on a plane again and never forgave himself for losing his wife and the family he'd wanted to have with her," Kyle finished.

"So he made you his family, instead," Emma said. "He thinks you're making the same mistakes he did."

"It would be nice if Bax would keep his opinions to himself once in a while."

Their feet halted at the foot of the wide steps leading up to the wide door. She looked at him. "I think the situations are completely different."

"You do."

"Yes. Although I agree with him that you work much too hard."

"Better this young man working hard than me," a voice greeted from the top of the stairs.

Emma swallowed nervously and looked up at the open doorway. An older man stood there, tall and distinguished-looking. Kyle settled his hand at the small of her back and they went up the stairs.

"Payton," Kyle greeted blandly. "This is Emma."

The man's eyes crinkled with his smile. "You're as lovely as I expected," he said gallantly. "Helen and I are delighted you and Kyle can join us this evening."

Emma started to relax. The older man was simply too gracious not to respond to. "Thank you for having us," she said, glancing at Kyle as Payton ushered them into the spacious home. He was smiling, too, but it didn't come close to reaching his eyes.

Kyle realized Emma was looking at him in concern. He deliberately relaxed his shoulders and smiled. But he knew she wasn't fooled.

Fortunately, however, Helen Cummings joined them and the rounds of introductions began. The older woman eventually slipped her arm through Emma's as if they were old friends and happily spied the photo album Kyle held. The women wandered away, leaving Kyle with Payton and several of the older man's golfing buddies.

Kyle responded with half his attention while they discussed the merits of various golf courses. He noticed that Payton's stepdaughter was also there. Winter made a beeline for Emma and her mother, who was smiling as she pored over the pictures.

Kyle nearly went over to rescue Emma. But when Winter left the group after a few minutes, her expression sulky, he realized that his lovely Emma needed no rescuing. Not this time.

He pushed one hand into his pocket and watched Emma. She wore a red dress that ended just above her exquisite knees. The square neckline and crisp linen followed her lovely figure closely, but was by no means tawdry. She looked impossibly beautiful and utterly confident.

"Makes a man proud to have such a lovely wife."

Kyle realized that everyone but Payton had scattered. "Yes."

"Helen told me she ran into you at the Buttonwood Baby Clinic. She's impressed with your devotion to your family. You know I like that in a man."

Inside his pocket Kyle's hand curled into a fist. "Yes."

The older man studied him for a long moment, his hazel eyes thoughtful. "We will meet tomorrow," he finally said. "Get this paperwork signed and done with. I've spent all my life making Cummings Courier Service what it is today." He looked over at Winter, who was pouring herself a drink at the marble bar in the corner of the elegant living room. "I wish I'd had sons to pass it on to, but since I haven't, I'm glad to be handing CCS over to you. To a person who'll respect my life's work."

Kyle's gut churned. But his smile was smooth as butter. He looked the older man right in the eye, inwardly cursing everything that Payton Cummings was. Including the company that would soon be his to do with as he saw fit.

"Darling, dinner is ready in the dining room," Helen said as she glided toward them, Emma in tow.

Kyle slid his arm around Emma's shoulders and smiled blandly as they followed the older couple into the dining room, where all the guests were chatting and laughing and finding seats at the long elegant table.

He and Emma were placed at one end, right beside Payton, who was at the head. Now that the moment was here, Kyle wasn't sure he could actually stomach so much as a bite. But hidden by the white damask tablecloth, Emma's hand covered his, and Kyle managed to get through the interminable meal without revealing how much he hated the man who sat at the head of the table.

"Kyle. What's wrong?"

Kyle didn't look up from the grease he was wiping from his fingers. When they'd arrived home from their evening with Payton and Helen Cummings, he'd been grateful that Emma had been immediately busy with Chandler. He'd changed clothes and headed out to the garage and the *Lightning,* assuming that Emma would simply go to bed, seeing how late it was.

Instead, she stood in the doorway, looking at him with concern and determination in her eyes.

"Just keyed up," he said truthfully.

She eyed him skeptically. Then she padded down the concrete steps and crossed the barn of a garage, ducking under the wing of the partially restored plane.

"You should have on shoes," Kyle muttered, seeing her bare feet.

"It's perfectly clean," she countered. "I think a person could eat off the concrete in here. Does Baxter wash it down weekly? Oh, my goodness, you *do* own a pair of jeans."

Kyle smiled faintly. "Don't have a heart attack."

"Sugar, I just might. You look real fine in those blue jeans. I think you ought to go for this look more often. Greasy white T-shirt. Very old blue jeans. You could give the cover of *Colorado Business Weekly* a whole new look."

Kyle shook his head and tossed down the rag he'd been using. He nudged Emma back toward the door. "You should be sleeping."

"So should you." She wrapped her arms around her waist and her yellow nightgown drifted around her toes. "Tomorrow's the big day. Dotted-line day."

"Yes." She wasn't leaving, so Kyle took her hand and pulled her out the door and across the moonlit flagstone walk toward the house. The night was clear and warm and utterly silent.

"I guess I should start packing, then."

He stopped. "What?"

She pulled her hand from his and tucked her glossy hair behind her ear. "Once your business deal is done, you won't have need for a wife anymore."

"You're in a rush, then, to get back to your little apartment?"

Her lips parted. Compressed. "I…well…that was the agreement, wasn't it?"

He couldn't deny it. "I think you should stay for a while longer," he said. "Just in case."

Her eyebrows rose. "In case of what?"

"Who knows?" He pushed his hands into his pockets to keep from reaching for her. Their night together in Denver had been exquisite torture. But here, in his house, he knew he would not have the absolute concrete reason to keep their lovemaking from reaching its full conclusion. Not with the box of condoms Baxter had mockingly placed in his nightstand drawer. "There's no need for you to rush back to your apartment," he said. "You're comfortable here, aren't you? Consider it a vacation of sorts. Or an act of mercy. Because you know that Bax will be brokenhearted when you leave."

"Baxter," she murmured so softly he barely heard. Her shoulders moved in a great sigh, then she looked up at him. Her hair slid over her moon-gilded shoulders and her eyes glistened like dark pools. "I'll think about it."

He nodded. He wasn't comfortable at all with the knots in his stomach at the notion of her leaving. But knew that as soon as the deal was done, as soon as his long-sought goal was achieved, his knots would ease. He turned and walked into the kitchen, flipping on the overhead light and holding open the door for her to precede him.

"I liked Helen and Payton," she said as she passed him. "They're very genuine, I think. I feel badly about our pretense."

"You always did," he said. "From the get-go you didn't like the deception."

She leaned back against the butcher block in the

center of the room, her hands curled around the thick edge on either side of her. ''Yet you felt it was necessary.'' She eyed him. ''Why is that, Kyle? I know all your explanations already. But it just doesn't fit somehow.''

''You're imagining things.'' He prowled over to the refrigerator and pulled out a beer.

''Am I?'' Her gaze followed him. ''Do you know that you didn't smile once this evening?''

''Yes, I did.''

She shook her head. ''Not really. Your mouth moved certainly. But when you smile, Kyle, really smile, your eyes show it, too.'' She pushed away from the island and walked over to him. She lifted her hand and smoothed her fingertip along his temple. ''It shows here,'' she murmured. ''You were not happy to be there. I was nervous about making some silly blunder, but you…sugar, you were not happy.'' She lowered her hand, her fingertips resting on her collarbone, and he realized she wasn't quite as certain as her words would have him believe. ''I can't help but wonder why.''

''I've been waiting a long time for this opportunity.''

''Which should make you happy, then. Your plans for CCS and ChandlerAIR are coming to fruition. Payton is delighted you'll be keeping his company intact, moving ahead with—''

''I'm not.''

Her words halted.

''I'm going to take it apart piece by piece and enjoy every single moment of it,'' he said deliberately.

"You mean because the company will really be part of ChandlerAIR now?"

"No."

She frowned. "I don't think I understand."

"When I'm finished with CCS, there will be nothing left of it to even remember."

"Why?"

"It doesn't matter."

Emma couldn't prevent an impatient huff. "Of course it matters. It concerns you, Kyle. Everything about you matters to me." She closed her mouth on a snap, feeling her cheeks flame. "This isn't like you."

"It is exactly like me," he said roughly. "This is what I do, Emma. It's business."

"No," she said. "There's something more to it. You're a builder, Kyle. An achiever. Why would you acquire CCS just to tear it down? That's not what you said you wanted it for when we first met."

"I lied."

She swallowed, nearly falling back a step. "Despite the fact that I'm wearing this ring of yours—" she raised her left hand until the diamonds on the wedding band glittered in the bright overhead light "—I don't believe you make a habit of deception any more than I do."

"You'd be wrong, then," he said, his voice flat. "Don't credit me with any finer motives, Emma. They don't exist. I will obliterate CCS, because it will be mine to do with as I choose."

She shook her head. "This is wrong, Kyle. You know it inside. That's why you're so... Oh, *tormented* is the word that fits, I think. The man I've come to know is not a man who can blithely obliterate another man's life's work!''

Kyle slammed his unopened beer bottle down on the butcher-block island. ''He's not just another man,'' Kyle said, gritting his teeth. ''Payton Cummings is my father.''

Emma's mouth parted. She backed blindly toward the kitchen table and pulled out a chair, sinking weakly onto it. ''Your father?'' she whispered. ''Your…birth father?''

''The man who claimed at dinner tonight that he had no sons to whom he could rightfully pass on his company.'' Kyle's expression was tight. ''Ironic, isn't it?''

She pressed her fingers to her mouth. ''He really doesn't suspect? Doesn't know you?''

''Kyle Montgomery, CEO of ChandlerAIR, is a far cry from the seven-year-old son who begged his father not to leave.''

''There must be some mistake. He was so…nice.''

''He's a bastard who left me and my brothers and sisters in the care of a woman who couldn't find her way out of a pill bottle. A man who didn't contribute one bloody dollar to our support, and, my sweet Emma, I assure you he had plenty of it to go around. When Sally died and the state tried to find him, the social worker learned that he'd legally relinquished his parental rights to us. He didn't want us. And now he's got the almighty gall to pick and choose who he does business with on the basis of their fine upstanding family values!''

Emma's eyes burned. ''PJ. Payton what? Junior?''

"Payton Kyle Cummings, Jr.," he said. "CCS *will* be mine. And I *will* do with it what I choose."

"You're going to tell him after the fact, aren't you?"

His jaw clenched.

"You think that will finally put the past to rest."

"I know it will. Don't bother giving me reasons to the contrary."

"I wasn't going to." She dashed her fingers across her cheek and rose. She walked up to him and placed her hands around his corded neck. "You have to do what you feel you must." She rose onto her toes and pressed her lips gently to his.

His hands came around her waist. "What's that for?"

She swallowed. Thought about the feelings she'd had for Jeremy St. James. He'd said he'd loved her. Had taken her virginity and her heart and given back nothing.

Yet she didn't even hate him for it. Not anymore.

She had Chandler because of Jeremy. She'd met Kyle because of Jeremy.

And the feelings that filled her entire soul for Kyle made everything pale in comparison.

"Because I love you," she said softly, then smiled faintly when he just stared at her, his green eyes searching. "And I know you don't love me, so stop thinking of a way to let me down gently."

"I have nothing to offer you, Emma. I could provide every material comfort, but you'd still be with a man who only knows how to work. Baxter's belief would be all too true. And I don't want to hurt you that way."

Aching sadness welled in her chest. "I told you not to let me down gently."

He sighed and tugged her against him. "I don't know what else to do."

She pressed her forehead against his shoulder. Felt his heart beating beneath her cheek. She closed her eyes tightly, willing the tears away for now. He didn't need them. She didn't want them. "Take me to bed, Kyle."

He pulled back an inch. Lifted her chin with his thumb until their eyes met. "Emma."

"I don't want your reasons why we shouldn't any more than you want my reasons why you shouldn't continue with your plan for your father's company. I just want to make love with you, Kyle." Her heart raced as she pressed his palm against her breast. "Don't you want that, too?"

He lowered his forehead to hers. "You know I do."

"Then take me to bed," she whispered.

Kyle hesitated and her heart quailed. But he swept her up into his arms and carried her out of the kitchen, stopping long enough only to snap off the overhead light.

He carried her up that wide sweeping staircase, and she didn't care at all that the carpet was arctic white. She only cared that she was in his arms. And for this night, at least, he was hers.

Behind the closed door of his bedroom, Kyle set Emma on her feet beside his bed. He tossed back the blankets and Emma moved around behind him, wrapping her arms around his waist, pressing her cheek against his strong back.

She tugged up the bottom of his T-shirt and flattened her palms against his abdomen. Then she found the button at his waist and popped it loose. "I mentioned that I liked you in jeans, didn't I?"

Kyle stood, still as stone as her fingers found the next button on his strained fly. "Yes."

"Mmm." She drew in a breath and he felt every luscious curve against his back. "Well, sugar, I like you even more out of them." Her voice was pure sweetness. Pure invitation. She tugged and two more buttons popped free. Then her fingers were tormenting him even more.

He turned and dragged her nightgown up her hips and off. It was still fluttering to the floor when the rest of his clothes joined them and he dragged her down onto his bed.

Her legs were satin smooth. Her breasts creamy and thrusting against his lips. And her hands were busy driving him to the edge of sanity. He swore under his breath and caught her wrists in his, pressing them above her head where they couldn't do more damage before he was prepared. And then he looked at her. Really looked at her.

Her lips, glistening pink. Her beautiful body. Her hands that rested above her head, palms up. Totally vulnerable. Totally his. But it was her eyes that ensnared him. Dark. Shimmering with emotion.

His heart ached, because the emotion in her eyes felt like a weeping kiss goodbye. "I don't want to hurt you." He meant more than the physical.

She didn't waver. "You won't," she promised. She drew up her knee, brushing it along his hip.

His control snapped and he reached for the nightstand drawer.

When he made her his, Kyle knew that no woman would ever come close to moving him as deeply as Emma.

And when he awoke in the morning, hours later than his usual five o'clock, he knew without having to get up and look that she was gone.

Her wedding ring sat on the nightstand beside the bed.

Chapter Fifteen

"I hear this is the best place for a guy to get a cup of coffee."

Emma turned, her heart stuttering. But rather than Kyle standing on the other side of the counter, it was Jake. She tucked her order pad in the pocket of her Mom & Pop's apron and reached for the coffee carafe, pouring a cup, which she slid in front of him. "Why are you here, Jake?"

It had been two weeks since Emma took Chandler and left Kyle's home. Even the rampant speculation about her and Kyle had begun to die.

During that time, she hadn't heard anything from him directly. Despite her desire to leave his home with nothing more than what she'd taken to it, she'd found her apartment filled to the gills with the nursery furniture that had been delivered that first week at Kyle's.

If that wasn't enough, the baby grand piano that had arrived shortly afterward meant she couldn't even unfold her sofa bed at night.

She knew she had to send it all back. She'd gone into her arrangement with Kyle to cover her debt to the hospital. To provide some measure of security for her son. Now that the arrangement was over, she wanted none of those things. She only wanted Kyle's heart.

It was the one thing she wasn't sure he realized he even possessed. He'd convinced himself that all he cared about was ChandlerAIR. And avenging the past by tearing apart the company founded by his birth father.

She looked across the counter at Kyle's brother, waiting for an answer. He tucked his sunglasses into the neck of his black T-shirt and slid a manila envelope on the counter toward her. "That's for you."

"What is it?"

"Look and see."

There was no hint in his eyes. Only a similarity in shape and color to Kyle's that made her hurt inside. She picked up the envelope and opened it. Two eight-by-ten photos slid out. Emma holding Chandler that day in the gardens at the Crest. And Kyle, impossibly handsome in his severe black tuxedo. A breeze had caught his hair, and he was focusing on something out of the camera's range.

She swallowed and slid the photos back into the envelope. "Thank you. Have you, um, seen Kyle?"

"Nope."

It was midmorning and the diner wasn't busy. Emma leaned against the counter. "You plan to, though."

He pursed his lips. "Can't say I do."

She touched the envelope. "You could've mailed these. You're in Buttonwood because you want to see your brother."

"What's he doing these days?"

She folded her arms. "I wouldn't know. I haven't seen him in nearly two weeks."

"You love him."

She didn't flinch. "Yes."

"So why aren't you together?"

"Ask him."

He shook his head. "My brother has moved on with his life quite well. He doesn't need people from the past dragging him down."

"For intelligent men, you two behave incredibly stupidly. I'd like to thump you both upside the head."

Jake set down his coffee cup, his eyebrows raising.

"Why do you think Kyle tracked down you and Trace and Annie?"

"He told you about us?"

"Yes, he did. He takes his family ties very seriously. Both the old ones and the new ones. Even if he doesn't want to acknowledge it." Emma touched his hand briefly. "He worries about all of you."

She glanced up automatically when the bell over the door tinkled. And felt the blood drain from her face at the sight of Jeremy St. James, standing there all tanned skin and golden hair and gleaming teeth.

She was vaguely aware of Jake turning around to

see who'd entered. Heard Millie, dear Millie, swear under her breath and march across the diner, saying loudly and ridiculously that the diner was closed just now.

Everybody knew that Millie's place was open every day. Rain or shine.

Jeremy simply stepped around Millie and approached the counter. "Hello, Emma."

The shock was fading quickly. Emma pressed her palms to the counter. "What do you want, Jeremy?"

He glanced around. The few customers who were present were all watching avidly.

"Perhaps we could discuss this more privately?"

"We have nothing to discuss."

"The baby," he said stiffly.

She widened her eyes. "What baby? If you're referring to my son, I believe we both know where we stand on that issue." She was giddily grateful that she'd left Chandler with Penny that morning rather than bringing him into the diner with her.

"It's a boy." There was a strange satisfaction in Jeremy's voice that sent a wave of unease through Emma.

"Go away, Jeremy."

He looked at Jake, who was listening unabashedly. "This is a private matter," he said, his tone dismissive.

Emma wondered what on earth she'd ever seen in the man. "Then you shouldn't bring it up in the middle of a diner," Jake said easily. "Emma, love, you want me to get rid of the jerk?"

The jerk. Tears stung her eyes because it was the

term Kyle had always used. "He's not worth it," she said thickly. "Excuse me."

She rushed past Millie and went into the kitchen. Scrubbed furiously at her cheeks.

Millie followed her. "That little…snot," she said furiously. "Coming in here, making you cry."

Emma laughed brokenly and hugged her friend. "I'm not crying because of him," she assured. "But if you don't mind, I think I'll take my lunch break now. Just until he gives up on whatever he wants and leaves."

Millie was nodding, walking with Emma to the rear entrance. "If he's not gone in an hour, I'll call Sheriff Wright and have him removed."

"The St. James family would love that," Emma murmured. "I'll be back before the lunch rush," she promised, and slipped out the back door.

Walking quickly, she crossed the street and headed toward the park. Rachel Arquette was sitting on one of the benches, her hands folded over the enormous swell of her pregnant tummy. "Getting closer?" Emma asked, smiling sympathetically.

Rachel nodded and pushed awkwardly to her feet. She tugged at her nurse's uniform, smoothing the maternity top over herself. "What's the lunch special at Mom & Pop's?"

"Chicken potpie or meat loaf."

"Sounds good."

"Which?"

"Both." Rachel laughed and headed back toward the clinic. "Make sure Millie saves plenty for me when I take my lunch break in a few hours."

Emma watched Rachel for a moment. She wondered if it was any easier for Rachel than it had been for her, being single and pregnant. But while everybody in town concluded that Jeremy had been the father of Emma's baby, conjecture had been ripe over who'd fathered Rachel's.

She took the bench vacated by Rachel and gazed at the pretty flowers lining the walking path. The sun was warm and she slowly relaxed, closing her eyes. The flowers were nowhere near as riotous as the ones in the garden at Kyle's home. But for a little while she pictured herself back in that colorful retreat.

How she missed Kyle! Missed the way he'd grab a bunch of grapes and absently pop a few into his mouth. Missed the way his eyes crinkled when he smiled and missed the way he held Chandler.

Why was it that Jeremy's unexpected presence made her feel that loss so much more acutely?

"Is this seat taken?"

Her eyes flew open and she pressed her hand to her heart. "Gracious."

Payton Cummings smiled down at her. "Didn't mean to scare the wits out of you, my dear."

Emma rose. "I'm surprised to see you," she admitted. "How are you?" For a man whose company had been bought and parceled into nothing, he seemed surprisingly content. Now that she knew who he was, she wondered why everyone on the planet couldn't see the resemblance between him and Kyle. Except for the eyes and Kyle's darker hair, the men were very similar.

"Fine. I brought Helen into town to visit with her friend who works at the clinic. I thought I recognized you walking over here." He nodded at her apron, which had the Mom & Pop's logo plastered across it. "Taking a break?"

Emma nodded. She wasn't sure what to say. Wondered what Payton knew and didn't know.

"How is your son?"

"Fine. Just fine. Growing very fast."

"Just wait," he said easily. "Soon he'll be wanting the keys to your car. I'd like to see Kyle's face that day. If you two have a girl, it'll be even worse on that boy."

Emma's smile stiffened. He didn't know. He couldn't. Because if he did, he wouldn't be standing here visiting with her as if there was nothing on earth he'd rather be doing. She looked over her shoulder and could see the front of the diner. It was entirely possible that Jake was still there.

Payton sat down on the bench and let out an appreciative sigh. "Helen was right about all work making Payton a dull boy. The best thing I've done in a long time was to sell CCS to Kyle. It was the only thing in my life for a long while until I met Helen and Winter. But a man needs more than his work."

Emma wondered if Kyle would be Payton's age before he realized that, too. She pushed her hands in the patch pockets of her apron. "Your wife said you were in New Mexico for a while."

He nodded. "I went there after my first marriage broke up." He frowned, staring into the flowers near his feet. "It was an unpleasant situation," he explained. Then his expression cleared and he smiled at her. "And one of the reasons I'm so particular about the people with whom I do business. Kyle is an admirable man. He already knows the things it took me a lifetime to learn. And he's a lucky man to have a lovely woman like you at his side.''

Emma felt ill. ''Mr. Cummings. Payton. I—''

The squeal of tires shattered the quiet morning. They both looked over to see a low-slung black car pulling up in front of the diner. Kyle climbed out.

''Good gravy,'' Emma said faintly, her eyes following Kyle as he rounded the car and disappeared into the diner. Jake, Jeremy, Payton and Kyle, all in one day. This was a recipe for disaster.

''Looks like your husband is in a hurry to see you.'' Payton rose and closed his hand around her elbow. ''Shall we?''

Emma swallowed and nodded, since there really was no alternative. They walked out of the park and crossed the street, Emma's stomach tightening with every step. Kyle had no idea that Payton was here. She wished there was some way to prepare him.

But there wasn't. And in bare minutes Payton was following her through the front door of the diner.

Emma's eyes immediately focused on Kyle, who was standing at the counter beside Jake. He held the two photos from the envelope in his hand.

Emma fiddled with her apron, not knowing what to say. Jake, however, said it all.

''Well, well,'' he said in a goading voice. ''Look who's here, PJ.''

Beside her, Payton went still. Emma glanced at him, then hurried across to Kyle. The muscle in his jaw twitched, and she put both her hands around his arm. Reveled in the presence of him. The strength. The scent. The sight.

"What are you doing here, Kyle?"

"Millie called me. She said the jerk was here bothering you."

Emma looked over at her boss, who merely shrugged. So much for calling Sheriff Wright. Emma wasn't surprised, though. Millie had made it perfectly obvious that she thought Kyle was Emma's very own Prince Charming and that it was just a matter of time before Emma was living in that house up on the ridge for real.

Emma wished she had Millie's faith. But there was more at work here than Emma's overflowing love for the man standing so tensely beside her. She didn't know what had happened about the CCS deal. All she knew was that Kyle felt like a coiled cobra beside her, and Payton was staring at the two brothers like he was seeing ghosts.

"PJ," he murmured. "And Jacob. My God." He fumbled with a chair, wrapping one hand around the back of it for support. "How can this be?"

Desperately torn, Emma looked up at Kyle. But his lips were tight and Jake looked no better. Payton looked ashen.

"Why didn't you tell me?" he asked. "Why, PJ?"

"My name is Kyle. Kyle Montgomery. There hasn't been a PJ Cummings since the day you walked out of our house and forgot we existed."

Payton shook his head, rubbing his shoulder with one hand. "No. No, son, it wasn't like that."

"I am not your son."

Payton frowned, his pain clear for all to see.

"I, on the other hand, am your son," Jake said

bitterly. "But I still hate your guts for abandoning us the way you did."

Emma looked from one man to the next. She understood Kyle's and Jake's feelings. But couldn't they see that Payton was suffering, too? She pressed her cheek against Kyle's shoulder, murmuring his name. He was unmoving.

She couldn't stand it. Payton looked as if he was ready to collapse. She let go of Kyle's arm and started for the older man.

She didn't reach him in time. With a grimace and a long low moan, he collapsed.

Emma cried out, rushing to the man. She couldn't find a pulse and she gently rolled him onto his back. "Millie!"

Millie was already heading to the phone. "Across the street from dozens of doctors and nurses," she fretted, "and not one of them in here when we need 'em."

Emma leaned over Kyle's father, but he wasn't breathing. Heart racing, she started CPR. Then nearly jumped out of her skin when Kyle crouched beside her. Her eyes met his and he grimly took over pressing his folded fist over his father's heart while Emma counted beats, then put her mouth over Payton's, breathing air into his lungs.

She knew it hadn't been long at all before the bell over the door jangled and the room was filled with medical personnel. But it felt like an eternity.

She moved gratefully aside when a doctor took her place. She pressed her fingertips to her forehead and backed out of the way, tugging Kyle to move, as well.

"That's Colt Rollins," she told him when he finally moved. "He's a wonderful doctor." She remembered the man from his time at the clinic. He'd been the one to confirm her pregnancy. But shortly after, Emma had heard that he'd left for a position in New Mexico.

Emma pushed Kyle toward an empty booth. "Sit down," she said softly. "Payton will be all right. Dr. Rollins will see to it."

Even Jake looked shaken. He walked up beside them, closing his hand over Kyle's shoulder.

Kyle tugged his tie loose and pulled Emma against him. She went willingly. She rested her hand atop Jake's and the three of them watched while Colt and two other doctors worked over Payton.

"Oh, my Lord," Emma said. "Helen Cummings is visiting her friend at the clinic. We have to find her. Tell her."

Jake started toward the door. "I'll find her."

"Does he know who she is?" Emma asked Kyle.

"Yes."

Emma's eyes followed Jake as he walked out the door. Then Rachel and another nurse caught Emma's attention as they arrived with a rolling stretcher, Rachel huffing and puffing and pressing one hand to her side. Emma glanced at Millie, who took one look at Rachel and shook her head, pointing to a chair. "You've got no business rushing around like this in your condition, missy. Now sit down."

Rachel, who did indeed look pale, sat. The doctors strapped Payton onto the stretcher and rolled it toward the door. Emma watched as Colt did a double take when he saw Rachel sitting there. He looked at

Payton, who was already being borne to the emergency room just across the way.

Rachel pushed to her feet. "I didn't realize you were back," she said to Colt, who was staring at her pregnant belly as if he'd never seen one before. Then he grasped her wrist and pulled her outside.

With Payton, Rachel and Colt all gone from the diner, Emma crouched in front of Kyle, her attention on him. "Are you okay? We could go to the emergency room and wait with Helen and Jake."

"I've hated Payton Cummings nearly as long as I can remember."

Emma didn't know what to say.

"But I realize that I don't want him to die." He scrubbed his hand down his face, then folded her hands in his. His green eyes focused on her face. "Are you okay?"

She nodded. "I'm worried about Payton and Helen." She pressed her cheek to his hand. "And you."

"That's not what I meant."

She raised her brows.

"The jerk," he said abruptly. "Jeremy. Millie called me to tell me he was here. He's not good enough for you, Emma. I thought for a while that, if you really loved him, I could stand it."

Emma shook her head and pushed to her feet, tugging at his hands until he stood, also. "He's gone," she said dismissively. "And the only man I love is you. Let's go across the street."

He didn't move. He was like an anchor, drawing Emma back toward him. "Why?"

"So we can see how Payton is, of course. The

doctors here are wonderful, so I don't want you automatically assuming the worst.''

''I thought you were the one who came out of the womb worrying.'' He pulled her into his arms, kissing her silent.

Emma could do nothing but respond. But her cheeks heated when she finally came back down off her tiptoes and realized that Millie was watching them, a wide smile on her face. She looked away, out the windows toward the clinic. Colt and Rachel were standing just outside. They appeared to be in fierce conversation.

Emma unwrapped her apron and left it behind the counter to Millie's easy assurance that she'd manage the lunch rush just fine. ''There's so much adrenaline pumping through my system,'' she said, ''it'll keep me going until three o'clock at least.''

Emma retrieved her purse and the photos Jake had delivered. ''Thanks, Millie.''

Her boss shooed her and Kyle out the door.

Kyle tucked her hand in his and they crossed the street.

Jake had obviously found Helen Cummings, because the two were sitting side by side in the small emergency waiting room. Helen jumped up at their entrance, her face worried. ''Kyle. Please. They haven't told me anything. Won't you see what you can find out?''

He sighed, gently nudging her back into a seat. ''Looked like a heart attack.''

Helen covered her mouth with a shaking hand. Emma sat down beside her and put her arm around her, comforting. "Kyle will see what he can learn," she assured her softly.

He nodded. Pulled loose his tie another inch and turned toward the desk where a nurse was talking on the phone. But he didn't have to wait long, because Dennis Reid strode into the waiting room. He stopped to speak to Kyle, then turned to Helen. "Payton is stable for now," he said, and they all sighed with relief. "He's conscious and demanding to see the whole lot of you. But I think you're enough for now, Helen. For the next day or two at least."

He waited for Helen to stand, then escorted her through the doors leading out of the waiting room.

"Guess it's safe to go now," Jake said.

Emma held her breath, looking from one brother to the other.

"There's room at the house," Kyle said, "if you want to hang around awhile."

Emma's shoulders relaxed.

But Jake shook his head. "Maybe next time." He smiled faintly. "I'll do some shots at Chandler's baptism," he offered.

Emma knew Jake was only being sweet. He could have no idea how his genuine offer pained her. But Kyle was nodding and shook his brother's hand briefly. "That'd be great," he said.

Jake leaned over and kissed her cheek. "Forgot to tell you," he said when he straightened. "I might bring a date next time." He smiled crookedly. "You'd both like her." He sketched a wave and strode through the sliding doors of the emergency room.

Leaving just Kyle and Emma.

Her eyes burned. "I should get back to the diner," she said after a moment. "Despite Millie's optimism, she *will* need help with the lunch rush." Realizing she'd brought the photos with her, she pulled out the photo of him and handed it to him. "Do you want it?"

"Not that one. I want the photo of my wife."

"Your pretend wife," she corrected. But she handed him the envelope that still contained the photo of her and Chandler. She was glad he didn't want the photo of himself, actually. She could frame it and keep it always. "Will you keep me posted on Payton's progress?"

Kyle nodded, his expression unreadable.

Emma picked up her purse, clutching it and the photo like a lifeline. "Well, everything is out in the open now," she said. "I hope you give Payton a chance to explain his side of things, Kyle. He admires you greatly, and he had no idea who you really were."

He didn't answer. Not that Emma had expected otherwise. "Give Baxter my best," she said brightly. "And, um, take care of yourself. Don't work too hard." Her voice wavered. She reached up and kissed his lean cheek, then hurried out of the emergency room.

Tears clogged her throat as she jogged across the street toward the diner. Millie took one look at her and told her to go home.

Emma gladly went, cradling Kyle's picture to her breast.

Chapter Sixteen

The moment Kyle got out of his car, he heard the music. He shut the car door softly and stared up the narrow flight of stairs to Emma's apartment.

She was playing the piano. And it was as soul-wrenching as it had been that night in Denver.

He climbed the stairs. Grimaced when he found the wooden screen door unlatched. But that didn't keep him from taking advantage of the unsecured door, and he quietly stepped inside. The apartment was stuffed with furniture from stem to stern.

The piano stood where her round dining table had once stood and was now nowhere in sight. Emma's back was to him as she sat at the piano and let her fingers drift hauntingly over the keys. Beside her on the floor Chandler kicked his legs, making his canvas seat bounce.

Kyle crossed the room, leaving the thick binder he'd brought with him on the couch before stepping around the crib and changing table. He crouched down beside the baby and tickled his chin. And grinned when Chandler's mouth parted happily. The baby jerked his feet even more enthusiastically.

Emma closed the piano, not surprised to see Kyle. She'd been aware of him the moment he'd entered the apartment. He'd obviously gone home since she'd seen him earlier, because he'd changed into those ridiculously sexy jeans and a soft blue-and-red polo shirt. "I called to check on Payton," she said. "He answered the phone in his room himself. I was surprised. But he sounded good."

"Colt Rollins ran tests. All in all they consider it a mild attack. No permanent damage to his heart."

"I'm glad." Her apartment was too close for words. First with the furniture, then, more disturbingly, with him. In the diner and even at the emergency room, things had moved so quickly, so frantically, there'd been no time for awkwardness.

But now, oh, now there was plenty of time. She stood and brushed her palms down the sides of her denim shorts as she scooted the piano bench in with her knee. "Would you like something to drink? Iced tea or...?"

He straightened. "No." He picked up the photo that Emma had placed on the top of the piano. "Jake sees a lot through that camera of his," he murmured. "He always did." He set the photo back on the piano. "I know the exact moment he took that photo. I was looking at you and Chandler. Jake must have looked, too. Because the second one he took showed exactly what I was seeing.''

Emma started to sit on the arm of her couch, but stopped when his intense eyes focused on her.

"It's as if he could see inside my head with that one photo,'' he said. "There you were. Beautiful in white. The loving mother. Everything I ever dreamed a woman could be, but didn't really believe existed.''

Emma swallowed. "Kyle—"

"Let me finish.''

She sat on the arm of the couch because her knees were simply too shaky to hold her up. "Finish away, sugar.''

He smiled faintly. "Not only did she exist, but she wore my ring. At least for appearances' sake. And at times she seemed to know me better than I knew myself. I am a builder, Emma. Just like you said. Not with wood or metal, maybe." He scooted out the footlocker and sat on it, his hands resting on his thighs.

It reminded her of the first day she'd met him when he came to her hospital room. Except this time he wore faded jeans and scuffed athletic shoes instead of a dress shirt and perfectly tailored trousers. But he still smelled like a fantasy come true. Except Emma knew that Kyle Montgomery was no fantasy.

He was a flesh-and-blood man, who'd overcome pain and loss and disillusionment to make a success of himself.

"I decided not to dismantle CCS," he said quietly.

Relief swept through her. "I'm glad. For you and for Payton.''

"Jake and Trace and Annie, too," he added. "I'm

making sure they've got equal interests in CCS. Everybody benefits.'' He was silent for a moment. Reached across the space between them and captured her hands in his. "He says he didn't know."

Emma didn't need to ask who *he* was.

"Not about Sally's death. Not about the booze or the drugs. He left because she blamed him for Janice's accident. Says he thought she would finally move on if he wasn't around constantly reminding her of the drowning."

"Do you believe him?"

"I don't know. I've spent a lot of years believing otherwise." He sighed. "But it was a belief I formed from what I knew as a kid. What Sally told us. God knows she wasn't the most reliable of sources. Payton says he kept paying child support into Sally's account, but that one day when I'd have been around eighteen his payments came back because the account had been closed. When he looked into it, he came up against a brick wall. We'd been gone for several years. PJ Cummings didn't exist. Jake and Trace and Annie were in other states.

"When I learned that Payton was back in Colorado, I knew I wanted his company, one way or the other. Chandler and Lydia would have known right off what I was up to, which is why I sent them on a cruise until it was over."

"You wouldn't have wanted to disappoint them," Emma surmised.

"Once you meet them—" Kyle grinned "—you'll know what I mean. Chandler wouldn't have been disappointed. He'd just have gone to Payton himself and demanded to know what the hell he'd been doing when his oldest son was stealing car radios to pay for food for his little brothers and sister. He's an up-front kind of guy.''

Emma was happy to hear it all. She truly was. But sitting there listening to Kyle talk as if she'd actually meet the rest of his family was too painful. She got to her feet. "I'm thirsty," she said. "Are you sure you wouldn't like something?"

He rose, too. "Emma, sweetness, I'm not here for iced tea.''

She closed her eyes for a moment. "Then what are you here for, Kyle?"

Emma frowned with dismay when she heard foot-steps pounding up the outside stairs. She pushed a hand through her hair and turned toward the door. It was probably Penny or Millie.

It was Jeremy St. James.

Emma stared at him through the screen door. She felt only irritation at his unwelcome interruption yet again. "Go away."

He pulled open the unlatched door and stepped inside. "Emma… Good grief," he stopped short at the sight of all the furniture packed into her small space. Then the corner of his lip curled distastefully when he saw Kyle. "I guess I can see what you did with the money," he said, turning his attention back to Emma. "Your tastes are more expensive than I'd have thought, darling. Here I gave you dozens of roses and it seems that furniture would have been more to your liking. Oh, that's the baby over there, I suppose.''

Emma stepped into his path when he started to cross the room. "You have no right to be here, Jeremy. Or is your memory so short you can't remember that?''

"Things are different now,'' Jeremy said confidently. "I'm married.''

"Congratulations. I'm sure you both deserve each other,'' Emma said. She would be forever grateful that she hadn't become Jeremy's wife. She'd rather have the brief time she'd had with Kyle than a lifetime with the weak Jeremy St. James.

"We've decided,'' Jeremy said, "that we'd like to raise the baby ourselves.''

Emma sensed Kyle coming up behind her. She was grateful for the hand he closed over her shoulder. If only because it kept her from going for Jeremy's throat. "If you come within five feet of my son, I'll—''

"My son, too.''

Emma shook her head. "Go home to your wife, Jeremy. I'm not interested in anything you have to say.''

"Emma, I'm not going anywhere yet.''

"She said get out.'' Kyle's voice was deadly soft.

Jeremy didn't have the good sense God gave a goose. He looked at Kyle and his lip curled. "She's good in bed, of course. Wild, actually. But you'll find she's expensive in the end. It took my parents fifty thousand to pay her off.''

Emma caught Kyle's arm before his fist found Jeremy's sneering face. Jeremy smiled, satisfied. Probably thinking she was trying to protect him or some such ridiculous notion.

"And what does the silly girl do? Goes out and

buys a bunch of furniture.'' Jeremy started to step around them toward Chandler. Kyle blocked his path.

Emma darted down the short hallway and threw open the closet door. She dug around in the box on the shelf for a moment and came back out just in time to see Kyle looming over Jeremy. She slipped between them, slapping a legal document against Jeremy's chin. ''Read it,'' she snapped, nudging Kyle back a few inches with a warning look. ''I can handle this,'' she murmured, then turned back to face Jeremy. ''Refresh your memory, you smarmy twit. That's your signature at the end of those twelve pages. You very clearly stated you were not responsible for the child carried by one Emma Valentine.''

''You took money in exchange for this document.''

''That's a lie!''

''My parents said you cashed the check.''

''Did they?'' She shook her head, leaning back against Kyle for support. ''I believe it would be more accurate to say that your parents made very generous donations to the Dooley Community Church in Dooley, Tennessee, and the Buttonwood Chapel and the Buttonwood Baby Clinic right here in scenic Buttonwood, Colorado.''

Jeremy's eyes narrowed. ''You wouldn't have.'' He waved at the baby grand. ''Where did all this come from, then? Darling, you've barely got a pot to your name.''

Kyle had had enough. Sure, Emma was more than capable of standing up to the jerk on her own. But she wasn't on her own; they were together. And if the jerk hadn't interrupted them, she'd realize that by now. He gently scooted Emma to the side, deftly slipped the legal document out of Jeremy's slack grasp and handed it to her. "Keep hold of that, sweetness. It might come in handy when I officially adopt Chandler."

Her eyes widened.

He smiled into her lovely eyes. Then turned to face the jerk. Now he didn't smile at all. "Emma asked you to leave."

Jeremy opened his mouth.

Then Kyle smiled. And wrapped his fingers around the younger man's throat, squeezing just enough to make the younger man's eyes bulge in fear. He walked toward the door, making Jeremy shuffle backward. When they reached the landing of the stairs, Kyle looked deliberately down them. "It's a long way to the ground, isn't it?" he said, and felt Jeremy's nervous swallow against his palm.

He lowered his hand. "Don't come back," he suggested softly. "Or I'll tie you and your family up in court for so long that whatever means you've got will end up in the hands of very happy, very wealthy attorneys."

"Now look here. I don't know who the hell you think you are—"

"I'm Kyle Montgomery," he said softly. Waited a moment until Jeremy recognized the name. "I made it my business to know all about you and the St. James clan weeks ago. And you *will* regret it if you cause my family one more moment of pain."

"Your family?"

"That's right." He glanced back at Emma, who

was sitting on the couch, cradling Chandler protectively in her arms. "My family."

"I'm not afraid of you, Montgomery."

Kyle shrugged, unimpressed. "That's your right, of course. But it's not me you should fear. It's Emma. Because she'll claw out your eyes if you come close to our son. And I'll take great pleasure in standing aside to watch. Then I'll feed you to her friends in Buttonwood. The ones who know how you treated her once you'd had your fun. Emma brings out great loyalty in people, you know. She's that kind of woman—with integrity. Then we'll make a trip to the bar association. They don't take kindly to law students who cheat on their bar exams."

Jeremy paled. "You wouldn't. I didn't cheat—"

"Who are they going to believe, Jeremy? You do have that incident on your record from your sophomore year in college. You know the one?"

Jeremy swore. "Fine. Forget it. She can keep the little brat. She always was more trouble than she was worth. Wouldn't even sleep with me until I told her I'd marry her. And then—"

Kyle shut both doors in Jeremy's face, cutting off his bitter tirade, and turned to Emma. "Now. Where were we?"

Emma rose, with Chandler still in her arms. "I'm sorry," she murmured. "I never dreamed that Jeremy would reappear and be so...unpleasant."

"That's not your fault, sweetness. I believe we were somewhere around here." He nudged her back onto the couch and sat down on the footlocker across from her. "As I was saying—"

"It was good of you to try to protect us," she interrupted. "But truly, I could have handled him."

"You did fine," he agreed. "And I know you don't need me, but I'm hoping—"

"I didn't keep the money, either," she added. "I truly did send it off to Dooley and to the chapel, and baby clinic here."

"I don't doubt that for a second."

"And I plan to send back all this furniture, Kyle. It's just not right that I've got it all. And the piano. Oh, I love the piano, just as you knew I would. But it's much too generous. And I really don't have the space—"

Kyle sighed and cupped his hand behind her neck, covering her mouth with his. She moaned softly, her words finally ceasing. He kept right on kissing her. It was an activity he'd become addicted to.

But Chandler squawked between them and Kyle sat back on the footlocker. "Be quiet," he said to both mother and son.

Emma's mouth opened. Then slowly closed. Chandler kicked his legs happily, little gurgles and grunts coming out of his tiny bow mouth.

"I meant what I said to the jerk," Kyle said. "You are my family. You and Chandler. I didn't say I wanted to adopt him to scare off Jeremy. I said it because I want it to be so. For me. For you. For Chandler."

Emma's heart squeezed. Then Kyle took Chandler out of her arms and settled him in his crib on the other side of the cramped room. "There's just gonna be times I want your mama to myself," he said conversationally. "Now and then." He returned to the footlocker in front of the sofa and handed Emma the fat binder he'd brought in with him.

She frowned, looking down at it. He opened it for her. Inside were small carpet samples and a rainbow of paint colors. "What is this?"

"You hate all that white in my house," he murmured. "As it happens, so do I. Add color to my house, Emma Valentine. Add color to my life."

A tear worked its way from her eye and dropped onto the book of samples.

"Remind me to look at the view," he continued, his voice dropping a notch. "To smell the flowers. Give me a reason to come home from the office an hour early. Or go in an hour late, because I'm too busy making love to my wife to beat every single employee into the parking lot. And play your beautiful music, sweetness. Because with you by my side, I can really feel it."

Emma looked into his eyes, feeling faint as that intense green gaze absorbed her.

"I'm looking for a wife, Emma Valentine," he said softly. "A real one this time."

Emma laughed softly and swiped the tears from her cheek. Kyle smiled, too. And stuck his hand in his pocket. His long fingers shook a little when he held out the diamond solitaire ring. It was as different from the glittering diamond-crusted band he'd presented that day at the Crest as a ring could be. No less beautiful. But much more suited to Emma's elegantly simple style.

He took her trembling hand and slipped it on her finger. "Let me be Chandler's father. Let me give him a houseful of brothers and sisters if that's what you want. I love you, Emma. Give me your heart. God knows you've both already got mine.''

She curled her hand around his and pressed it to her, then slipped into his arms with a soft cry. ''It is yours, Kyle. I love you.''

He rose, pulling her with him. ''Then you'll marry me?''

She nodded, blindly seeking his mouth with hers. ''Yes. Anytime you say. The sooner the better.''

He laughed, low and exultant and so masculine that she melted inside even more.

''We could elope,'' he suggested, his eyes full of love and desire. He lifted her right off her feet, and Emma wrapped her arms around his strong shoulders.

She chuckled, delighted and weak-kneed and plumb crazy about him. ''Well,'' she said, her voice honey smooth despite the giddy bubbles dancing in her chest, ''we do have the wedding photos already taken care of.''

Their eyes met. ''So we could head right on into the honeymoon,'' he finished.

Emma smiled slowly. ''Oh, sugar. The way you think.''

''Oh, Emma, honey,'' he drawled right back at her. ''The way you love me.''

Her lips curved. ''Did I ever tell you how much I love the way you smell?'' she whispered against his ear.

Kyle smiled, then shuffled them toward the couch and pulled her down over him, filling his hands with her dark glossy hair. Filling his heart with the love shining from her eyes. "I won't ever stop loving you," he said.

She went still. Then she laid her palm against his jaw and kissed him, impossibly sweet. Impossibly desirable. "Neither will I, Kyle, my love. Neither will I."

Their lips met.

In his crib across the room, Chandler gurgled softly. When nobody rose to dote on him, he kicked his feet a few times. Then stuck his fist in his mouth and sighed with satisfaction.

*   *   *   *   *

*Here's a sneak preview of
Laurie Paige's compelling story,*

MAKE WAY FOR BABIES,
on sale next month.

*Spence McBride and his best friend Ally had
shared a soul-shattering kiss on their school
graduation night...and then they went off to
college and went on their separate ways.
When Spence returned home, Ally was engaged to
his brother, Jack. But now that Ally was a widow
with newborn twins to nurture, Spence felt
heart-stirrings he'd long denied. Would tiny twin
matchmakers named Nicholas and Hannah
help bring together two hearts that were always
meant to beat as one?*

Make Way for Babies

by

Laurie Paige

Spence McBride remained in the maternity wing's waiting room while little Nicholas and Hannah were bathed and put in a warmer—he imagined something like a chicken incubator with dozens of babies tucked into their little individual pockets. His widowed sister-in-law Ally had gone with the nurse to help with the twins she was adopting while his mom, Rose, stayed with Taylor, the babies' birth mother.

Spence sipped the bitter coffee from the machine. Ugh. It was hard to take on an empty stomach. As if by way of a gentle reminder, his stomach growled.

"Yeah, yeah," he said.

Ally bustled into the room. "Hi. Talking to yourself? Better watch it. That's the second sign of senility."

"What's the first?" he asked, going along with her

teasing mood even as it made him remember days gone by.

"I forget," she said, then burst into laughter.

Listening to her husky voice with its intriguing little breaks, he laughed too. She'd always had the ability to make him feel better. When she was in an exuberant mood, as she was now, she was prone to laugh and tease unmercifully.

But she had also listened…in those long ago days when they were friends—before she had married his brother, before Jack had been killed.

Spence tossed his coffee cup into the trash bin. "How about dinner? I haven't eaten since breakfast."

"That would be great. Taylor and the babies are asleep, so it would be a good time to go. I'll get Rose."

He nodded, but she was already gone, a whirlwind of energy, shining radiance on all who came into her orbit.

His heart pounded suddenly. The birthing had caused some strange twists in him that afternoon. He hadn't realized it would be so emotional and affecting.

And now, after the kiss Ally planted on him in the birthing room had seared him right down to the soles of his feet—well, he kept thinking of other things, about things he hadn't let himself think of in years.

Ally returned and stuck her head in the door. The hall light turned her blond hair into a golden halo around her slender, oval face. Her hair always looked tousled. Her cheeks were always pink. As if she'd just come in from some fun exercise in the outdoors. Or climbed out of bed. His body stirred hungrily.

For a second, he considered what it would be like to share the excitement of bringing a new life into the world with a beloved mate. And the excitement of creating that new life. Heat seared through him. At one moment, when he was there in the birthing room holding the two babies, an image had flashed through his mind—of him and a woman and their children....

"Ready?" she asked.

"Yes." His voice was husky, sexy. He cleared it. "Yes," he said again, more firmly this time.

Yeah, it was a good thing that his mom would be with them tonight.

* * *

Look for the rest of the story next month

▼™ SILHOUETTE
SPECIAL EDITION®

AVAILABLE FROM 19TH OCTOBER 2001

MAKE WAY FOR BABIES! Laurie Paige

That's My Baby!

Spencer McBride hadn't ever been able to resist Ally, and now she was alone with adopted newborn twins the confirmed bachelor was considering the role of father...lover...husband?

EXPECTANT BRIDE-TO-BE Nikki Benjamin

Here Come the Brides

Jack Randall had always been Abby's protector and after one fruitful night of passion, he was determined to do the right thing. If he could get Abby to pose as his fiancée, then it was only a short step to the altar!

LARA'S LOVER Penny Richards

When Donovan Delaney was imprisoned for a crime he didn't commit, he unknowingly left teenager Lara Grayson pregnant and desperate. Now Lara's lover was back in town...

HER LITTLE SECRET Joan Elliott Pickart

Lindsey Patterson and Cable Montana agreed to act as lovers to keep the town's matchmakers happy, but they didn't forsee the plan's huge hitch...falling for each other!

GOOD MORNING, STRANGER Laurie Campbell

Mick's memory had completely vanished, but his male instincts were in perfect working order—and insisting he kiss Annelise Brennan senseless. But what did he have in common with her...love?

THE VIRGIN BRIDE SAID, 'WOW!' Cathy Gillen Thacker

The Lockhart Brides

The only way for Kelsey Lockhart to hold onto the family land was to become partners with Brady Anderson—in business *and* in bed. For Brady wanted a *real* marriage...

1001/23a

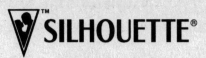

Silhouette Stars

Born this month

Julie Andrews, Don McLean, Chubby Checker, Sir Terence Conran, Bob Geldof, Britt Ekland, Margaret Thatcher, Roger Moore, Sarah Ferguson, John Le Carre.

Star of the month

Libra

The year ahead starts slowly and you may feel frustrated by your lack of progress, but the pace will quicken, and indeed the opportunities that arise may lead to a complete change of lifestyle. Romance is highlighted and you could find yourself making a stronger commitment to your relationship.

SILH/HR/1001a

 **Scorpio**

You should be feeling energetic and able to achieve all that you want. Some friendships could be proving to be more trouble than they are worth. However, they could surprise you late in the month.

Sagittarius

Recent events may have left you wondering who you can trust – relax, as all is about to become clear and you could be impressed by someone's motives. Finances improve and you could enjoy a lucky break mid-month.

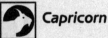 **Capricorn**

After a quiet start to the month the pace quickens and you should make real progress. The home front, however, must not be ignored as someone may feel neglected.

Aquarius

Recent celebrations have brought you back into contact with old friends and you now have the chance to renew your social life. A small health problem should clear up quickly.

 Pisces

Having a firm idea about what you want to achieve is only half the battle. You need to communicate and get those close to you involved if you are to succeed. A friend may let you down but hear them out before condemning them.

Aries

A go-ahead month with new opportunities arising in many areas of your life. Socially you are in demand and a chance meeting could lead to an interesting situation.